love,

Michelle + Paul

THE BOYS

AND THE BUTTERFLIES

THE BOYS
AND
THE BUTTERFLIES

A wartime rural childhood

James Birdsall

PAVILION
MICHAEL JOSEPH

The Author would like to thank Mrs Jocelyn Starling for her kind permission to reproduce one of the late Timothy Birdsall's hitherto unpublished drawings, and Mr Robin Ford of Messrs Watkins and Doncaster (the Naturalists) of Hawkhurst, for an evocative photograph on which to base a sketch of their old shop in the Strand.

First published in Great Britain in 1988 by
PAVILION BOOKS LIMITED
196 Shaftesbury Avenue, London WC2H 8JL
in association with Michael Joseph Limited
27 Wrights Lane, Kensington, London W8 5TZ

Text and illustrations © 1988 James Birdsall

British Library Cataloguing in Publication Data
Birdsall, James
The boys and the butterflies.
1. World War, 1939–1945 —
Personal narratives
I. Title
940.53'092'4   D811.5
ISBN 1 85145 185 4 Hbk
ISBN 1 85145 294 X Pbk

Phototypeset by
Wyvern Typesetting Ltd, Bristol
Printed and bound in Great Britain by
Butler & Tanner Ltd, Frome and London

Jacket photograph reproduced by
kind permission of The Photo Source Limited.

This book is dedicated to the memory of the artist,
Timothy Birdsall.
Tim was cartoonist for the *Sunday Times*,
political cartoonist of the *Spectator* and
unique illustrator of his own monologues on the
once controversial BBC Television show,
'That Was The Week That Was'.
He died of leukaemia in 1963.
He was twenty-seven.

CONTENTS

PREFACE

Often, when young, would I vow that, in the event of my one day having children of my own, never would I preface a remark with 'Now, when I was your age . . .' Alas for crumbled good intentions! Like everyone else I succumb to the innately conventional. The difference is that I have a *conscience* about it; as soon as a glib 'Of course in my day . . .' or a patronizing 'Now you won't remember the wartime, but . . .' has escaped me, I murmur a mute, guilty apology to an earnest small boy, still around but stifled, who once dreamed he could flout ancestral lore and avoid the mistakes of his elders.

This really is why I have written a book. I used to think then, wistfully or in exasperation depending on the circumstances, why can't they write it all down? Then one could dip into it when in the mood instead of having it thrust upon one. I still think it's a good idea. Now that I am indisputably the 'eldest' and all the others have gone, there are so many questions I want to ask them about people they remembered and I don't. So I decided to put my pen where my mouth was and preserve what I can for the younger members of the family to look at in the days to come when they become interested, as they surely will, and when I have forgotten or can't be bothered. It might, too, stop me saying, 'Now, when I was your age . . .'

It was only after this that some nice and manifestly discerning people decided that a lot of others might be interested as well. Two irksome problems confront me when setting all this down, due no doubt to the Yorkshire half of my ancestry. For the Yorkshireman and, even more, the Yorkshirewoman are preoccupied with two things above all others: accurate chronology, and exactly how everybody is related to everyone else. You know the sort of thing:

'Now I'll not see him again while Thursday for he was here Monday. I'm a liar – I was on wi' wringer all morning Monday, 'appen it were Tuesday. Aye, Tuesday, it must have been. Or was it Monday? . . .'

And the favourite Yorkshire game of Happy Families goes on even longer. Both preoccupations can hold up a good anecdote until you've long forgotten the original subject:

'. . .and he were just dragging her corpse past Mrs Braithwaite's gate – you know, Thirza Braithwaite – she was a Metcalf before she married. Aye! Alma Metcalf's lass – and she'd have been a Sidgwick, I think – Old Ashley would be uncle to her, and who did he marry? Let me see . . .'

J. B. Priestley didn't invent Time as the Sassenachs suspect, he inherited it as a Yorkshireman. He came to the conclusion that Time exists all together in the same instant. It's as though we were all sitting in a cinema, watching events happening one after another. But somewhere up at the back, the projectionist can take the film out and hold it up and peer at any section of it he wants to, because it's all there, every frame. Fiction is easy – you simply arrange events to suit yourself. But my story is made up from scraps lying about on the cutting room floor of my untidy memory and I am often hard put to it to say what place in the sequence they originally occupied. So it's a story full of flashbacks. And flash forwards.

The second difficulty has its roots in the habit of providing children with battalions of aunts and uncles who have no consanguine perch on the family tree at all, merely friends of Mum and Dad. If you are confused, so was I. I don't remember when the three of us first sat down and deliberated who was really related to us and who wasn't. I do remember that many of the dreary ones were and some of the more exciting, to our sorrow, were not. I have tried to sort out the tangle by the use of inverted commas for our adopted 'aunts' and 'uncles'. I hope it helps.

This is not a book for people who know everything about butterflies, any more than it is a book for people who know everything about small boys. But the butterflies were so inextricably interwoven with our lives, that not only is it impossible to pull them out, like tares among the wheat, but they seem to have taken over and the title should be the other way round. The book, I realize, is neither one thing nor the other and 'that's just the trouble' (as Tim would have said). Still, I can't ignore a persistent small voice which asks provokingly, 'Why can't it be both? At once?' So that's what it is. Present reference books will tell you that there are sixty-one different species of British butterfly. Of course in my day . . . but you had better read the book.

Jas Birdsall
Yorkshire 1987

The Village

1. The Old Rectory
2. The Church
3. The White Lion
4. The Rectory
5. The Red Lion
6. Forge
7. The Robin Hood
8. The Cottage

9. The Searchlight
10. The Village Green
11. Cider Brewery
12. Village School
13. Old Mill
14. The Strawberry Field

One Mile

CHAPTER ONE

The Young Evacuees

The inglenook

I T must be very rare, we decided, if it had not yet got into the butterfly book. The family had been spending a sunny afternoon in the Little Woods, a baby plantation which lay to the south-east of our little Hertfordshire village, picking wild strawberries for jam. Our first 'butterfly' was in fact a day-flying moth. Tim caught it in his hands. Later we found out it was called a 'Cinnabar' but at the time we just marvelled at its beauty – the startling vermilion red of the hindwings contrasting with grey-black forewings with a stripe of the same red. Tim put it in a matchbox and took it home. We had a small *Observer's* book of butterflies among countless books on natural history and we scanned the pictures, but nowhere was there anything like our lovely specimen.

That night Tim took a Momentous Decision. 'I'm going to start a butterfly collection', said Tim. The year was 1941. I would have been six, Tim five and Patrick a stalwart three-year-old.

We kept the decision from Mum. She would, we felt, point out – quite fairly – that we had too many collections already. Most small boys get a collecting bug but we three were infested. There were birds' eggs, mostly the inherited accumulation of two generations before us but added to occasionally when a new species was discovered. We were dedicated conservationists though we had never heard the word. As later with the butterflies and moths, we understood, I think instinctively, that nothing should ever be taken indiscriminately; we knew that the location of a nest was a jealously guarded secret; we knew that birds lost count after three or four but would miss one egg if there were only two. The shame of possibly causing a bird to 'desert' would keep us awake at nights. The relief to return the next day and find she was still sitting!

We collected rockery stones. These were the grotesque, lime-covered flints found in the numerous chalk pits, knobbed and hollowed, often holed through the middle, as though some gnome-like Henry Moore had been sculpting underground for thousands of centuries past. The rockeries were full of them in the garden and the paths were lined with them where other, less adventurous gardeners would use bricks or those austere little iron hoops, and still we brought more. 'Only interesting shapes,' we would remind each other, 'we've really got enough!' But there was always a new, an even more fascinating shape whenever we climbed down a chalk pit and so the collection kept growing. The pits are all filled in now, I see, and obedient ranks of wheat brown where the boys burrowed and the badgers lived and the yellowhammers wrote our initials on their monogrammed eggs. (The yellowhammer was known by country people as the 'Writing Lark'. Its whitish eggs were covered in blotches and spidery scrawls as if some palsied hand had been at work with a mapping pen. We each had an egg with a 'J', a 'T' and a 'P' respectively.)

At least rockery stones were kept outside. Other flints – arrow heads, axes, anything that our wishful imaginations could turn into a stone-age relic – swelled the contents of the nursery shelves which already held the appearance of an eccentric museum. I collected zoo animals and Tim collected battleships. I had HMS *Hood* and was appalled when it went down. Tim, with *Nelson*, *Renown* and *Rodney*, was luckier at the time but I had lost my heart for battleships.

The contents of Patrick's pockets were a collection in themselves. He would spend whole afternoons absorbedly collecting 'wums and sniles'. Most of Patrick's collected treasures went into the water butt – the real gems he took to bed with him, like the ermine stoat we found dead in a trap in St John's Wood (pronounced 'Sinjuns'). Too soon, the 'gaminess' of his bedfellow gave him away and it was removed, much to his indignation.

Regimental cap-badges and other military souvenirs were another growing department. Uncle Arthur was a pilot in the RAF. Uncle John had joined the Army in New Zealand where he had been farming. So we had shell cases and a real bush hat with one side rolled up and even a strange, black German altimeter which must have come from an aircraft during what we all then called the 'last' war. I used to point out that it could not have been the last war as we were having another one now, but it was explained to me that it meant the one before, not the final one. This one would be the last one. And, indeed, so it is now called. The irony was lost on me in those days.

Patrick had an imaginary soldier friend called 'Lemby'. Tim and I accepted Lemby without any surprise or disbelief and discussed him and his uniform as though he were a real part of the family. He was totally real to Patrick. Occasionally a strange tin-hat would be hanging on the hall stand, or a khaki vehicle parked outside the Cottage. 'That's Lemby's', Patrick would say casually. We never demurred. Cousin Jane had a friend called Penny-Ann who was an irritating nuisance in that she had to have a place set for her at table –

even, on London visits, in Whiteley's restaurant in the gallery of that huge, baroque department store in Kensington, where we always went after sitting on rocking-horses to get our hair cut. To our amazement, the grown-ups seemed to take this very seriously. We wondered, Tim and I, why Lemby never came to lunch. 'He's always away somewhere, fighting and things', was the totally logical explanation. Inquisitive adults would often ask Patrick where Lemby was. 'Somewhere in England', he would reply mysteriously. It was where the factories were when we listened to 'Workers' Playtime' on the wireless and it sounded suitably official.

We had come to our little Hertfordshire village a year before, in May 1940, at the same time as the dazed remnants of the British Army had been snatched away from Dunkirk. When the war started we had left London. We had a house in Cambridge Gardens with a lift up the outside that the toys used to ride in to get upstairs from the garden, but we were never allowed to. My parents' bedroom door had an emerald green porcelain handle. It was just on a level with my nose. I first met Patrick in that room in 1938. I had been staying in Yorkshire with my grandparents and had ordered a little sister called Sally. They had got it wrong. I tiptoed up to the cot with people standing around, strangely watchful like 'When did you last see your Father?' in Madame Tussauds. He let out a squall of shattering power and I dived through legs for the green door knob and escaped. I am still wary of his capacity for the unexpected.

Gas fires and darkening evenings and the bell of the muffin-man. I don't remember much about Cambridge Gardens except Littlewoods in Ladbroke Grove which smelt of tarred string and biscuits and a forest of signs like frozen flags, saying TO BE LET OR SOLD. That was when we left.

We moved to Eastbourne where Mum had an army of aunts and cousins and Tim and I went to school. I remember deep snow that winter, even in Eastbourne, and losing Tim in a drift on the way to school. Only his ginger cap showed on the top and a kind man came and hauled him out like pulling a leek. We never did find his gumboots. One afternoon we all walked up on the Downs. This was marvellous, as Mrs Vernon, our charlady, only took us round the cemetery to look at her relations who were all white stone ladies with wings. We rolled a huge snowball and pushed it over the cliff and then we sat and watched the sun go down like a huge, red apple. Dad said something which must have been about whether we would ever see this again, because it was very melancholy and I enjoyed it hugely. I didn't know that one day I would know every hollow and gorse bush and hunt for Small Elephant Hawk caterpillars in the lady's bedstraw where the snow lay in 1939. A few months later we could hear the guns across the Channel. When things 'looked bad in France', we moved away from the coast and stayed for a while in Caxton in Cambridgeshire.

Caxton had a real gibbet in front of a pub (it still has) and we stayed with a doctor friend and his wife and their son called George. George wore a top hat like John Darling (he can't have worn it all the time, I suppose) and was older than I. We had a splendid time sticking strips of gummed brown paper criss-cross all over the windows. Life was steeped in sunshine and strawberries and the exciting smell of tomatoes in the greenhouse. I envied George his top hat. Then one day up rolled a rustic taxi and out stepped my grandparents. We were going to be evacuees.

Skipton had begun to absorb children from the threatened cities who were evacuated for their safety. My grandparents, worried about our safety because Dad, a consultant surgeon, had to be in London, decided to look after their own. Gramp had been playing dominoes with a friend, a widely famed character of the Dales who was both taxi driver and an avid collector of 'foongi'. (He pronounced 'fungi' as a Yorkshireman would pronounce 'funny' if he had no roof to his mouth.) This expert mycologist had travelled the kingdom in search of foongi and knew Caxton well. Thus was organized the longest taxi journey he had ever undertaken and the three evacuees were carted excitedly up to the West Riding out of danger. The cost must have been trivial by today's standards, but it impressed me, used to London taxis as an expensive indulgence, enormously.

Then began another chapter in collecting. My grandfather was a highly respected optician, angler and naturalist, a Freeman of the City of London, a formidable authority on Dickens and, in curiosity, as childlike as myself. He took collecting seriously as thinking people should and entered into the spirit of the thing with an enthusiasm that took your breath away. I wanted to know what a mouse skeleton looked like. We had found some prize owl pellets with bones sticking every which way out of the grey fur and I wanted to know where they fitted on the mouse. We procured a convenient mouse (they were continually being trapped – in the pantry, in the garden and in the allotment), and when everyone else was out it was duly skinned and boiled in a tin on the fire. Sniffing like the Bisto Kids, we both agreed the flavour was quite appetizing as the stew spread its fragrance around the kitchen. And owls obviously found them delicious. When we judged it soft enough, it was brought out, cooled, and the meat carefully dissected away and lo, we had the skeleton we sought. The rest was a question of matching ours to the bones the owl had discarded. Later we found it caused less criticism from the womenfolk to leave our corpses on a convenient ants' nest. The work was done for us. To express an interest in anything was, to my grandfather, a mere prelude to buying a book about it. Sure enough, the next evening duly saw the arrival of a blue-backed volume, *Practical Taxidermy*.

Years later, I made some reparation for the encouragement he always gave me, when he sent me a beetle while I was up at Cambridge. He had found it crawling down his neck when he was splitting logs. It was still alive when it reached me – a green, slender fellow with enormously long antennae and it squeaked. I showed it to the then President of the University Boats, an 'aggers' man and a fellow eccentric, who took it to the Professor of Entomology in the Agricultural Faculty, who coveted it. It was a very rare beetle. The only record they had was a tiny, shrivelled specimen from back in the last century. I confess, to my shame, that I cannot remember the Latin name, beetles being one order which eluded my catholic collectivism, but I presented it to the Cambridge collection provided that the name of J. Ernest Birdsall of Threshfield was recorded for posterity as the captor and donor. The old boy was tickled pink.

Practical Taxidermy was a revelation. The chapter on mammals advised you to start with a substantial animal. The book started with a fox. I started with mice. I had often watched my grandmother skinning rabbits in the kitchen, but the preliminary was the chopping off of ears, feet and tail. Gramp would tie the tail on to a length of string and thread it up his coat sleeve. We were invited to stroke the little, fluffy tail protruding from his cuff, whereupon it would twitch in apparent fright up into the sleeve. I had fathomed the working of the trick early on but it was still hilarious in repeat performances.

Now, the legs had to be turned inside out carefully and the skin removed, like getting out of your breeches and stockings without taking your boots off. All the little girls who lived in the immediate neighbourhood had dolls' houses. Soon the dining rooms were proudly sporting field vole rugs and trophies of shrews and house mice whose heads were mounted on tiny plywood shields over the mantelpiece. I never managed to cure them effectively, as the preservative pastes recommended contained noxious substances like mercury and arsenic. These, I understood, had been responsible for the Hatter's madness. I had to make do with saltpetre. When the ornaments got too high I replaced them.

Tom Pickles kept a barber's shop in Sheep Street, complete with the spirally striped pole. He must have been one of the last of the true Dickensian barbers, as he sold cage birds and mended umbrellas as well. We'd sit on high stools with vast sheets wound round us and have our heads clipped all over, 'down to t'wood', to the accompanying chirrups of canaries, goldfinches and bullfinches and Tom whistling tunelessly down the backs of our necks. He had also been a taxidermist. Gramp told me that when Dad was a small boy, he and a friend, in the course of a feud with Tom Pickles, had turned up with a dead parrot, predating John Cleese by some forty-odd years.

'Do you stuff birds?'

'Aye, lads!'

'Then stuff this one – down yer throat!'

All my grandfather's stories had to be true as he always showed you the place where the incident had happened. Haircutting was the one subject where we were in total disagreement. He had about as much hair left as the average grape but still went every week to have it cut. We would return from Yorkshire to the distress of my mother, shaved all over like young delinquents bound for Botany Bay.

We returned to the South when the Cottage became ours, and we eventually moved into it in the May of 1940. Our village lay inside a triangle, the points of which were formed by three splendid butterfly woods, with a fourth on the perimeter. I put this in the past tense, for at least one magnificent oak wood has been destroyed to build the sprawling Stevenage New Town, and another (the Little Woods) has matured to a dark cathedral of conifers where little else grows. St John's Wood was about a mile to the east of us. Box Wood was roughly the same distance to the west, with High Wood a mile and a half to the south. What we called the 'Little Woods' were half way on a line between St John's and High Wood. The little village (as it was then) boasted four pubs and a cider brewery. We slept in the White Lion for a bit while days were spent at the Cottage cutting lino into strange shapes and looking for secret passages. The bar of the White Lion (there was a Red Lion almost opposite and we felt, vainly patriotic, there should be a Blue to make up the trio) was too high to look over. The porch outside the stable-like half door had been built with wide seats to accommodate three small boys and their glasses of fizzy lemonade. The main source of trouble manifested itself at night. The only sanitation was an ancient two-hole earth closet down the garden. The dual nature of the seat struck us as eminently sensible. There was a large, man-sized hole and a smaller one for children and dwarves. It made for company in a situation which was normally rather a lonely one. At night, however, there was only the jerry. That in itself was no hardship – everyone used them in those days – but if this one required emptying (and in particular circumstances such could be imperative) the only route it could take to the outside was through the crowded bar. Upstairs we could hear the cheers and ribaldry that marked its progress and Mum would be furious with the incontinent offender, as it was always she who had to run the gauntlet.

The Cottage was to be part of us during most of the formative years of our childhood, and I can still hear the distinctive noise of every door latch and feel the texture of every separate beam. Originally built in the late sixteenth century, it had remained virtually unchanged until plumbing and electricity had been installed shortly before we were. A large inglenook had been discovered, bricked up as it stood, and the glass in the latticed windows and the tiles on the floor were centuries old. It had no secret passage. One upright beam must have once been a warship's timber, as a deep crack had been spliced with a crudely cut ship's saw. The central chimney was so wide that it shone like a vertical beacon when a fire was roaring in the basket below, and a 'valve' of two slates was inserted to comply with the blackout regulations. A vertical pillar of oak supported the main cross beams in the middle of the 'lounge'. On it was ritually carved, every birthday, the heights of the Birdsall boys, and I often wonder if this tally, with its 'J's and 'T's and 'P's has caused some speculative curiosity in the minds of the new owners.

The three of us shared the nursery. On the ceiling of the dining room below there developed three long cracks in the plaster, the visible betrayal of that forbidden delight, bouncing on beds. Patrick had a solid oak cot, massively built by Mr Carter, the joiner and builder who was helping with the Cottage. It needed to be solid. The nursery blackout had unexpected by-products. Blackout was achieved by wedging rectangles of plaster board into the window frames. The board was covered with the blackout material then in general use and 'off coupons'. The inside was faced with the same material as our Mickey Mouse curtains to make it less austere. We went to bed early, in the height of the afternoon, it seemed, for those were the days of 'Double Summer Time' so scorned by A. P. Herbert, who didn't see why the Nation couldn't just get up two hours earlier. The sun shone until late at night. A tiny chink must have appeared somewhere in the blind, because one night after lights out, we saw projected, to our astonishment, the bulky figure of the postmistress cycling slowly and ponderously, upside-down, across the ceiling. After that, on sunny evenings, we enjoyed our own private camera obscura and the lazy drama of village life – or that fragment of it which was enacted on a fifty-yard stretch of the road outside – silently and topsy-turvily unfolded itself above our beds.

It wasn't very long before I found out that we were spies. Invasion was imminent and spy-fever was at its height. We had a car. Not only did we have a car, but we had petrol to run it. Dad disappeared on a Monday morning, came back briefly late on a Wednesday night to disappear the following morning and returned on Friday night. This was suspicious in itself. Men would be surprised on their tummies trying to look under the kitchen door. I think the prevailing theory was that Dad was the spy and the poor little wife knew nothing about it. None of the neighbours enlightened her. But their children told us three.

I felt uneasily guilty. Tim and I went to a little private school in Stevenage and we played picture lotto – in German, no less! Tim reassured me that lotto was a German game and couldn't be played any other way. It wasn't all that convincing and I have never been to a Bingo Hall to this day. A few months later the school went bust and we went to the Village School where we learned far more and spoke Hertfordshire. This seemed even more unpopular than German with our parents, though we were quite unaware of possessing any accent at all. I was dimly conscious that James rhymed with Grimes (*The Water Babies* was a favourite at the time) and that Grimes rhymed with

9

Poimes which were found in Poitry books. Strange phrases and idioms were much more apparent. 'You ain't half sharp, oldun!' was a wary greeting as with two strange dogs. Most things were little and old. I remember a gushing woman gazing into another's pram. 'He's a lovely little-old baby!' she bellowed at the tiny, wrinkled occupant. I took the 'lovely' with a pinch of salt, but the rest was unarguable.

We entered into the spirit of the spy-catching with enthusiasm. Dad had now become established as a patriotic practitioner and was known to most of the customers of the White Lion as 'Doc'. This was hardly a title to impress the Royal College of Surgeons, but Doc was, we knew, the most authoritative and paternal of the Seven Dwarves and this gave it a ring of respectable authenticity. A few later newcomers had arrived in the village and suspicion was diverted to them. Near St Albans a spy had been caught when he stole a bicycle and rode off on the right-hand side of the road. He'd had invisible ink on him. In our village everyone rode their bikes plumb down the middle of the road. How on earth could you tell if someone had invisible ink on him?

Asking the way was a sure sign of espionage. All the signposts had been taken down and burnt so the Germans would get lost when they invaded. We often got hopelessly lost in the car and as for British convoys, they must have been regularly missing presumed dead. The name of our village had even been blacked out on Mr Berry the policeman's house and it now read ONSTABULARY. That really would disconcert the Nazi invaders. Tim said that the Germans were an hour ahead of us all the time. So we followed our quarry furtively around all day and regularly asked them the time. Soon we had logged their watches over a week or ten days. Those who couldn't tell us the time were doubly suspect. What the objects of our scrutiny thought about our apparent obsession with the time of day, I shudder to think. One even more sinisterly inconsequential incident stands out from a London visit. We were walking down Harley Street with Dad and a woman stopped us and asked the time. 'Half-past eleven', said Doc, consulting his watch.

'Oh no, it's not, you know,' said the woman triumphantly, 'it's gone twelve o'clock.' Perhaps she was M.I.5.

We didn't get around much by ourselves in these early days and it was not until the following year that Tim caught the Cinnabar moth that was to change our lives. By that time most of the air raids would have stopped. During the Battle of Britain and the later Blitz, our world was more or less bounded by the confines of the village green, known to some as 'The Wreck', which I could never fathom, conjuring as it did images of Ballantyne and the Swiss Family Robinson. The large green was just across the road from the Cottage so we were retrievable when the sirens went. They had held the fairs there in the past and the house next door to ours was called 'Fairview'. They tried to call us 'Fairview Cottage' but the name never really stuck. Years later they tried to call us Number Something High Street. That never got as much as a foothold – I can't even remember the number.

The village green had swings and a seesaw and a sort of maypole or giant stride where a girl called Sylvia got so entangled the wrong way up that she had to be cut down. A particular sweetheart of mine, a little Cockney evacuee called Mavis, used to sit with me on the swings and we would share a stick of rhubarb. After she had had a good chew we would trot over to the pump and give it a brisk wash. Then it was my turn. Hygiene in Eden. The pump – there were several dotted round the village – was a tubby, cast-iron one with a handle that you turned like a large door-knob. Most of the poorer villagers were not on the mains water supply and this was their only source of fresh water so there was usually someone there filling a bucket. We even found these pumps out in the woods – marvellous on a thirsty day's butterflying. There was a hawthorn, its gnarled branches forming seats and perches polished smooth by generations of corduroy backsides, which served as a council chamber or a climbing frame or a Wellington Bomber. There was also an air-raid shelter, called The Dug-out. It was a deep tunnel with steps down at either end, full of waterlogged clay and hundreds of frogs who spent their days there jumping clammily about, blissfully immune to the onslaughts of the Luftwaffe. I never heard of any people using it during a raid.

Daylight raids were quite fun once safely indoors. Outside it was much more frightening. The cold terror of black and white crosses on wings was intensified when you actually saw the pilot. It never occurred to us that he was too bent on escape to machine gun small boys as they ran for home down the High Street. We were thirty-five miles north of London, and although we had many airfields around us, the fighters that came over had probably lost their way. Bombers would drop their loads to lighten the plane and this was dangerous, but most of the bombs merely left craters in the ploughed fields where we would excitedly go and investigate the next day. At home during air raids we had special places to sit and special drawing books which only came out on such occasions. This was where the fun came in.

My book I grandly entitled *Memories*. I can't have built up many memories at that early stage of my life, but, by Heaven, I was going to remember what they were! And the extraordinary thing is that I still do. I don't know whether it is a common experience among artists, but on examining any painting I have ever done, I can recall the circumstances of its creation. Still in existence is a painting of mine of the inglenook, with the log fire blazing. I know I was listening to Arthur Askey in a pantomime on the wireless at the time. I remember the pantomime was Aladdin. When I look at the painting and retrace how I tackled it, I can recall actual lines of dialogue. The best 'memory' was a pastel drawing of a dormouse which we disturbed, furious, outside its nest in the Strawberry Field (a part of St John's Wood with an overgrowth of undergrowth).

Tim's book was filled with people mostly (airmen especially) who even then had that vibrant life with a few pencil strokes which was later to make him familiar to millions of people in his newspaper cartoons and on 'That Was the Week That Was' on BBC Television. It also had lots of pictures of Us–doing–heroic–things. Tim had a theory that he wasn't really our brother at all but an important young prince who was being brought up with us incognito for safety. This modesty got the sort of rough reception one would expect from his two common-blooded foster brothers and the changeling was mercilessly scragged.

The nearest they ever got to us was during an afternoon raid when an incendiary bomb came down in the back garden. The inglenook was built solidly of brick and overhead was a kind of black steel ceiling with little traps in it which opened to the flue. With this armour plate and the huge brick chimney, we were told that nothing short of a direct hit could damage this central part of the house. As the thumps and bangs came rapidly nearer, we all huddled round the fire basket, empty in summer. We held hands convulsively. It had to be us next. The climax was a loud, wailing child's scream. As the bangs continued, but fading, Mum looked wildly across the lounge for Patrick, thinking he had fallen down the stairs at the far end. No, all three of us were wide eyed in the inglenook. Tension was broken by the A.R.P. hammering at the door. Men in black tin hats were up the garden emptying sand bags on to the bomb, a very small one about the size of a cocoa tin, and it had not exploded. It really had sounded like Patrick's regular wail as he tumbled downstairs.

Night raids were worse, but any menace is worse in the dark. You could recognize German bombers by the curious slow throb of the engines. A continuous drone was reassuring. It meant it was 'one of ours'. At weekends there was the rightness of everybody being there and somehow nothing could happen to us if we were all together. Dad would come back from cribbage when the sirens went and spread a comforting miasma of pipe smoke and beer. On Friday nights this was mixed with ether as he had been operating all day and his breath became mildly anaesthetic. We boys would be dressed hurriedly and down we trooped to our hearth and shelter. Tim and I curled up and often slept in the two oak seats recessed into the wall either side of the fire. Patrick was installed on the couch with Mum. This became a fairly regular routine, but there weren't many nights when we didn't go to bed upstairs at all. On weekdays Mum's anxiety was infectious. Dad would ring up from London every evening at six o'clock. I think we had some sort of priority due to his being a doctor, but it was often hard to get through. If the phone failed to ring on time the tension would become acute. We could hear all too well the London raids thirty-five miles away and at night there were the most amazing fireworks displays to the south. I am sure this had a lasting effect on me. I am still frightened by telephones and will find any excuse to avoid using one. The sirens on radio or television send shudders up my spine but the strident telephone bell is far worse.

The raids generated an unaffected camaraderie among everybody all the time which in later years we found was reserved for Christmas time only. When the nights got particularly noisy, people would process in and out to see that we were all right, knowing that Dad was in Town. Mr Bayes the Butcher, a large, jolly man who did his own slaughtering just over the road next to the green and bred greyhounds, would bundle in out of the night in his Warden's tin hat and shiny black weatherproof as we lay listening to the bombs and making pictures in the glowing embers of the log fire. This involved a titanic struggle with the blackout curtain from which he would emerge, panting, like some rotund black moth from a cocoon. 'Sounds bad over Lunnon. People say it's the Docks. They won't go for the West End. Everyone safe?' The lights would be switched off and Mr Bayes would bundle out again into the dark, leaving a courageous glow of security behind him. Our shopkeepers seemed to come straight from a pack of 'Happy Families'. There was also Mrs Bayes the Butcher's Wife and Mr Cannon the Cobbler and the grocer was Mr Kitchener which seemed appropriate enough, though we felt it lacked the proper alliterative ring.

We made regular visits to London, though we rarely spent the night there. Tim and I were top to toe in a camp bed in Harley Street the night John Lewis was hit and we were flung out on to the floor. The front wall of the store stayed up for a long time, a huge façade with no glass in the windows like a Hollywood film set. It was eventually pulled down and the foundations of the building housed exhibitions. It was there I remember seeing the first terrible photographs of the Horror Camps. Many of the bombed sites became temporary reservoirs. Long, flattened crosses painted on the walls bore an 'E' and 'W' in the left and right angles and an 'S' below. I later learned this stood for 'Emergency Water Supply' but at the time I vaguely thought of them as points of the compass – another lasting heritage as I still have to think carefully about the relative positions of east and west, which were, of course, the wrong way round.

The Polytechnic News Theatre in Regent Street was a favourite treat, with its large models of Walt Disney's characters in the foyer. A notice used to flash on the screen when the sirens went but nobody ever seemed to leave the cinema during a raid. You went out 'where you came in'. I remember far more about the cartoons than about the news with the urgent, cheerful commentators and brassy background music. The one with the double-lens camera which turned and looked at you – I think it was Movietone, or perhaps it was Gaumont British – used to worry me. I thought it was an enormous cannon and I hated staring down that menacing twin barrel. We didn't really know any film stars in those days, though Ethel, who looked after us, used to go all soppy about Robert Taylor's moustache.

The wireless had far more impact on our lives. The windows of the Harley Street consulting room overlooked the back of the BBC building in Portland Place. We used to stare at each blank window in turn wondering which one Tommy Handley was behind. The consulting room had a leopard on the floor called Wallace shot by Great Uncle Cyril in India. There we would have tins of kidney soup heated in the sterilizer. When patients were in we were banished downstairs to the waiting room, a silent Brobdingnag of leather chairs and mahogany furniture and musty magazines. But in one corner was a glass showcase. In the case was a branch and on the branch were stuffed humming birds and an array of moths and butterflies, wings outstretched in the position, never adopted in life, where their markings could be shown to the best advantage. Most of the species were 'Foreign'. This classification loftily embraced the hundreds of thousands of species of lepidoptera which were neither residents of nor visitors to the British Isles. But there was one Milkweed or Monarch Butterfly, found in all the books as a very rare migrant. All the glass that had fallen from John Lewis and this case remained impregnable! We spent hours staring at the Milkweed, dreaming up impossible schemes for extracting it from its Victorian tomb. It is probably still there.

Paddington Green had a statue of Mrs Siddons. I thought it must be Polly Perkins, though she looked a bit tragic. It was also the site of the Children's Hospital and we spent many happy hours there while less robust children were having their tonsils removed or their ears examined by Dad. The main hall was tiled with immense murals of Tenniel's illustration of the Mad Tea Party and other Victorian nursery favourites. The hospital became the pediatric unit of St Mary's when the National Health Service assumed sweeping command and it lost its individuality, but in those days it had a unique charm. The nurses were all known by their Christian names and probationers started at the age of sixteen. Nurse Peggy was a favourite of ours. She later became Lady Florey when her husband was honoured for his work on penicillin. Matron was a tall, lean Scotswoman, dressed to the ankles in black with incredibly stiff white cuffs, a very grand old lady. I adored her. She introduced me to Greek Mythology with an illustrated book called *Transformations*. I would trot along at the hem of her gown as she moved about her duties around the wards with patient authority, never raising her voice. Down in the warm cellars they grew exotic fruit to supplement the rations and vitamins for the children. Most of the wards were moved down there to be safe from the bombs, as the nearby railway station was a popular target. The operating theatres were upstairs, however, and would often be busy with casualties all night. One night Tim and I left Paddington Green with Dad in a taxi, having waited for a heavy raid to subside. I remember Dad remarking to the driver that it seemed a particularly bad night. 'Oh, I dunno, guv'nor,' replied the cabbie, 'it could be raining!'

Friends and relations would come to stay at the Cottage most weekends, relieved to be out of London for a while. They didn't have it too easy in the country, either, as our idyllic life involved an enormous amount of gardening and logging. We were more or less self-sufficient concerning vegetables and fuel, and guests would be mercilessly put to work. Some never came again. Most people loved it. The slave labour department (us) had no choice. The large garden at the back was a mass of tangled bindweed, horse radish, brick, rubble, clay and chalk. The residual signs of previous cultivation were the fruit trees; apple, plum and syrupy greengages beloved of the Red Admirals who got quietly tipsy on them. The trees were old, but magnificent croppers. Mum would get extra sugar on our jam coupons for bottling and jam making in season. Wartime jam was mostly turnip anyway. Behind the garden was a small jungle of snowberry bushes through which we tunnelled and made dens. Behind were fields and fields of grazing pasture. The Birdsall boys were ordered over the back fence every morning with two buckets and one spade apiece. 'A coople o' bookets o'moock' was the first chore of the day. The cleared garden was trenched down. Each trench was lined with cow manure, filled in and the next parallel trench dug. Dry cow claps were light and the work easy, but we had to go increasingly further afield to find them. New deposits were far heavier but not so far to carry. The relative advantages were an absorbing topic of debate. Patrick displayed his customary application when his imagination warmed to a new pursuit. Cart horses passed the Cottage all day. Such tractors that there were had no petrol so the Dobbins and Blossoms were an important part of the local work force. Horse was even better than cow. Patrick lurked by the front gate with his shovel and bucket, alert for windfalls. Ours was the cleanest bit of frontage in the village. This method, however, relied too much on the caprice of the passing animal, so when 'Them Two', and by this he meant his elder brothers, were at school, he would spend his mornings stolidly following the carts. Kindly farmers would give him a ride back with his spoils.

'Auntie' Sheelagh and 'Uncle' Farquy (short for Farquarson Small) were regulars. They had met originally at the Old Vic under the rigorous eye of Lilian Baylis, where Farquy was a producer and

Sheelagh had played all the small boys and princelings in Shakespeare. She had romped on the back of many an illustrious Richard III. By 1940 Farquy was a BBC producer whose predictable nickname was 'Talkerson Big'. When he was posted by the RAF, 'Auntie' Sheelagh would come by herself. She was minute and dynamic fun and my favourite 'aunt', a cousin of Mum's. She was Letitia Lamb in Toytown and Tiny Tim at Christmas and Uncle Mac was a great friend of hers. She had also played Peter Pan in the West End for many seasons and had her wrist broken in the fight on the pirate ship by Charles Hawtrey as Hook. She travelled half-fare on trains in a gym-tunic until she was about thirty. She was unbelievably naive about the countryside and we used to tease her without quarter and scare her witless with our ghost stories. Sparrows roosted under the eaves above our heads and we could hear them restlessly shuffling about well into the small hours. We invented an old miser who could be heard scrabbling after coins lost down the cracks between the floorboards. We did have a genuine ghost whose footsteps could be heard from downstairs pacing the floor above. Happily, he was never heard when you were upstairs and we got used to him and never worried. Another lodger was *Tegenaria domestica*, the Hertfordshire spider. The huge females, whose legs would easily span a saucer, were often trapped in the bath. They were quite harmless and we would pick them out gently and take them outside where they could run as fast as we could walk. They had a disconcerting habit of appearing on the bedroom ceiling. If you turned the light out and quickly on again, the monster would still be motionless, but had moved a few inches from where you last saw it. 'Auntie' Sheelagh spent one terrified night with the light on and thereafter summoned us to remove the malevolent spinner whenever one walked the ceiling.

Her greatest performance was played among the mushrooms. We were keen mushroom gatherers and we lived in good mushroom country. Our chief rival was Mr Justice, a distinguished, friendly gentleman who hid a cunning ruthlessness behind this mask when it came to mushrooms. Many times we would set off with our baskets only to meet him returning with his, full to the handle and an empty field behind him. He lacked our familiarity with dried cow dung, however, and this was his undoing. This versatile material was placed over mushrooms that were too small to take. Each hiding place was marked with a twig stuck in the ground a couple of paces away. A warm night and a heavy dew and we could wrest mushrooms from a field seemingly devoid of them. Such was the setting for the big tease. We persuaded the gullible Sheelagh that the only way to find mushrooms was to get up very early in the morning and tiptoe about in rubber boots. If they heard you coming, they would immediately pop back into the ground again. This ritual was duly observed, like Prospero's elves with printless foot, while the mist still lay on the grass, Sheelagh unable to suppress the occasional squeak when her excitement overcame her. The cow dung caches convinced her entirely. These, she reported at breakfast, were the ones which she had scared with her squeals and which the boys had just succeeded in pulling out of the ground again before they got away.

Another mushrooming incident comes to the surface. We always took sticks with us for walks. Manifold were their uses; probing in the undergrowth for mushrooms, decapitating thistles, preliminary investigation of holes in tree or bank, long handle for the butterfly net and general poling along of self when the legs complained. A white dome like a large marshmallow gleamed from a hundred yards away in the next field. Under the barbed wire slipped Patrick and he was half way there before we had stirred. Admittedly our hesitation had much to do with the other occupant of the field – a muscle-bound brown stud bull with serviceable looking horns and a ring in his nose, lying contentedly chewing the cud in the sunshine. Patrick held the prize mushroom aloft and one or two satellites which were growing around it. If we shouted to warn him it would wake the Minotaur! Triumphantly he headed back to the fence. If he came back on the same straight line, all would be well. But no, not Patrick! As the anxious spectators watched, impotent, he changed his course towards the hind quarters of the somnolent bull. Such indolence should not go uncontested when the rest of the world was up and doing. 'Get up, you lazy cow!' cried our young demagogue, giving the rump steak area a resounding thwack with his stick, and then came on. The bull, conscious, like Pooh-Bah, of his inordinate pedigree, turned his head slowly and shook it slightly with a low grumbling murmur (I swear it was 'Oh my protoplasmic Ancestor!') and turned back, peacefully, to chewing the cud.

As children, we took the war very much for granted. Tim and I missed bananas; Patrick had never really known them. He got fresh eggs on ration while the rest of us made do with the powdered variety.

Not content with this official bonanza, he would eat Tony Cat's liver and lights left outside the kitchen door. Tony Cat was our evacuee from Eastbourne. Aunt Ella, doyenne of the Great Aunts, had stayed in Eastbourne – no jumped-up Austrian corporal was going to move her – having given all her huge collection of Indian brass to make shell cases (unfortunately they probably made the fortune of some racketeer) and even the railings round the garden. The oldest surviving sister of my maternal grandfather (he had had seven and was the youngest of the family, the only boy) she was a formidable old lady. She was fondly proud of us three but seldom allowed it to show; tall, slender, a beauty, they said, in her day, and straight as a ramrod. She had two companions, Chin-Chin, a large, surly Peke, and Tony Cat who was a beautiful Persian Tortoiseshell tom and quite a rarity among pedigree cats. She had a family of Tommies billeted on her as well, whom she disciplined with a fairly benign autocracy as befitted a retired headmistress from Simla and staunch upholder of the British Raj. She listed their wives and sweethearts as personal relatives, conditional on the troops' good behaviour, and thus enabled occasional illicit visits of loved ones to the beleaguered coast.

All the aunts spoiled their animals rather than their children. They all had special sinks in their kitchens marked 'Animals Only'. This habit of putting up notices for animals to read struck us as Quixotic but proof of kindness at any rate. On the front gate of Capel House at the top of the village was a beauty which said, DOGS PLEASE USE TRADESMEN'S ENTRANCE.

Tony Cat was driven berserk by the shells and bombs. With no railings left to pen him in, he would disappear for days on end and was in danger of imminent breakdown. I suggested on the phone he should come to us as our evacuee. Aunt Ella jumped at it – metaphorically of course, for such betrayal of excitement was quite beneath her. So Tony Cat duly came with a label round his neck just like other evacuees. Dad was not enthusiastic (bird men never make good cat men). 'No pampering. He'll not get his own meat ration if he comes to us!' (He was right – Patrick got it most of the time.) On his first night Tony Cat was ejected amid howls of mortification from the boys who had been casting lots as to which bed he would snuggle up in. The next morning Tony Cat was mewling round our ankles in the kitchen. Mum, who had a weakness for corny scripts, said, 'I think he's trying to tell us something!' We followed him out to the garage door and there, laid proudly side by side like a good day's bag of salmon, were eight of the biggest rats ever seen, tails pointing south. The evacuee had proved his worth at a stroke and Mr Meade the Baker next door was delighted as the pests had come from the granary. Thereafter the results of every night's hunting were presented for morning inspection. Once admired and the hunter congratulated, they disappeared – where, we never discovered. Were we away for the weekend, three nights' ratcatching awaited us at the garage door when we returned. Tony Cat went back to Eastbourne in due course and resorted to his cosseted life, but I'm sure his big game hunting stories, grandly embroidered, were long destined to bore any staid companion he managed to buttonhole on the respectable Eastbourne roof tops.

Tony Cat had one enviable privilege: he didn't have to carry a gas mask. We had to carry ours everywhere. Quite a fashion built up in gas mask cases, as in handbags. Wearing them, we all looked like long-snouted piglets and you could make farting noises by breathing out and holding the cheek flaps down. Gas practices were announced by the Gas Rattle. It was only a football rattle, once, I believe, issued to the Police to supplement the whistle. It struck a particular terror through me. They used real tear gas at times to catch out people who had got casual about carrying their gas masks, and I had a small crack in the acetate window of mine. I passed the standard test – being able to hold a postcard on the base of the respirator by breathing in – but I knew that mine was but a useless decoration. I preferred to gamble on the unlikelihood of a real gas attack rather than face the wrath to come by admitting I needed a new gas mask. It was a constant anxiety, but the gamble paid off and by the spring of 1941 we began to suspect that the Nazis weren't going to come at all.

CHAPTER TWO

First Encounters on the Wing

Gatekeepers

I T was in the spring and summer of 1942 that our preoccupations became narrowed and focussed predominantly on butterflies and moths. The previous late summer had inspired a mere dilettante flirtation but now there developed a prolonged love affair with all its hopes and enthusiasms, its agitation and disappointment. The air raids were past, or at any rate the unceasing Blitz, and we were allowed to roam as far as our legs would carry us. Such distance was regularly miscalculated as we were forever scolded for being late back. The war had left us for Africa, for Malta and even India and although we, as children, were aware of it, it was there as a broad backcloth to life, no longer a direct, personal danger. Wistful images like 'peacetime' and 'pre-war' were ever in the conversations of our tired elders, but signified to us no more than the annoyingly unspecific 'happy-ever-after' epilogues to all fairytales. Christmas and birthdays were far more real, and really we had known nothing else, save khaki and urban drabness contrasted with rustic freedom and a bucolic laissez-faire which allowed the wild things to thrive while men concentrated on their own survival.

Those early days of butterflying were crammed with excitement, each one bringing new experience and new species. First, however, we required the tools of the trade. Old net curtains were dug out and three nets were run up for us on the sewing machine. Stout oak branches with a fork at the end served as handles and thin hoops of hazel were threaded through the curtain hem and fixed in place with staples. They were heavy nets and the hoops needed constant repair, but they were splendidly serviceable for beginners who knew no better. Our little book gave instructions into the mysteries of 'mounting' or 'setting' – the process by which the butterfly is pinned into the position that displays its wings to the best advantage. For this we needed a 'setting board', a long cork board with a groove down the centre to take the body of the insect. The same material which made the blackout blinds made our first clumsy setting boards, for these were wartime days of improvisation when margarine masqueraded as butter, sausages owed more to the baker than the butcher and young naturalists had to rely on their own – and their parents' – ingenuity. The (dead) specimen was impaled with a pin through the thorax and stuck in the groove in the setting board. The wings were then coaxed flat into the position where the base of the forewing – the trailing edge in aircraft terms – was at right angles to the fuselage, and the wings were finally clamped with pinned wedges of postcard to keep them flat. Later we used strips of celluloid from old X-ray film to pin the wings down – a useful perk of the medical profession.

Another medical perk supplied the killing bottle, for this is, of course, a tale of slaughter and sudden death. I can neither hide the fact nor escape the censure which must be levelled today. The reader who cannot envisage each capture without wincing should consign this book to the dustbin and go no further. Though I never dispatched a specimen without having to stifle a feeling of compunction, there is little I can say in mitigation which does not sound like indefensible excuse. Certainly the moth and butterfly population was far higher then than it is today and the indiscriminate greed of agriculture is vastly more to blame in this than the acquisitive instincts of three boys. The Jekyll and Hyde personality of the naturalist is an enigma common enough. Indeed, Dad used to go wildfowling with dedicated conservationists, Sir Peter Scott and Eric Ennyon, in their Cambridge days. It must also be said that most of the butterflies that we caught would have fulfilled their task for posterity. Few females start to fly far abroad until they have laid fertile eggs and established the generation to come.

Our first killing bottles were made from a screw-top jar lined with diced laurel leaves, which gave off the bitter almond smell of prussic acid. Such a lethal chamber does not retain its power for more than a few hours, and we soon graduated to cotton wool soaked in ether. This often had the disadvantage of soaking the occupant as well, but it was quick, merciful and effective. Eventually we came to the cyanide jar. A solution of potassium cyanide is covered with plaster of Paris and enough gas permeates the plaster to give a lasting atmosphere inside the jar. I'm sure no chemist would make one up for me today, but Rogers of Beaumont Street, dispensers to the medical élite behind a stout fortification of sandbags, treated it as an everyday part of their trade. It was never questioned by our parents that we were responsible enough to be trusted with these dangerous materials once the perils had been clearly pointed out.

Thus equipped, we set out, rather self-consciously at first but this was soon dispelled by the thrill of the chase. We had been aware of butterflies before, but there is a world of difference between merely seeing them and really looking at them. As we walked through the long grass, liberally scattered with scabious, cornflowers, red poppies and purple thistles, clouds of butterflies would rise, flap lazily about and then settle again. Most of these were brown, but among them were sparks of sapphire. The Common Blue was, as a name, a disappointment. 'Common' was a disparaging term used about table manners and idioms of speech which did not come up to scratch. But the Latin name was *icarus* and he was an uncommon pioneer of flight even though he did fly too near the sun. There was nothing common about this pretty butterfly except his tendency to brawl with others contesting his right to a particular flower, like a robin on a birdtable. And when he closed his wings – we would often find them sleeping, two or three to a stem – the underside was an intricate mosaic of spots and rings of orange and black on a dove-grey background. Unless you knew, you would not recognize the blue flier. His lady was dark brown with a hint of dark blue, bordered with orange rings and just as attractive in her way. An effective trick of the Blues, one that many butterflies have developed, is to close the wings suddenly during flight when they are pursued. Your eyes are desperately following an erratic blue spark which suddenly disappears. If you are especially alert, you may pick up the blue again where it has 'jinked', like a wing three-quarter, in a different direction, but many times the vanishing trick has you fooled completely.

We referred to a new bible, W. E. Kirby's *Butterflies and Moths of the United Kingdom*. To our consternation he listed eleven different Blues. We would have to examine our catches more closely. Clifden Blues and Mazarine Blues and even the Silver Studded Blue all seemed fairly similar from the pictures. It would be more difficult than we thought. But wait – a sinister paradox in the text: '[The Mazarine Blue] has been extinct for about thirty years. It appears in June and July.' W. E. Kirby wrote his colourful book some time in the last century, and he always softens the blow of an extinction by telling you when the species is likely to appear. The other relative of the Common Blue which we found early on was the Brown Argus (the many eyed) – a handsome, lively little butterfly, just bigger than your thumb nail. The male is brown like the female, with a string of rubies bordering the wings, fringed in white. The typical underside, however, puts him unmistakably in the same tribe as the Blues.

I remember lucidly our first Brown Argus. It must have been in the late summer of 1941 and Tim and I were in a field behind the garden

while Patrick was busy with one of his absorbing private games in the
snowberry bushes.

'Come on, Patrick, we've got a new one!'

'Can't!'

'Why not? What're you doing?'

'Makin' Slow Gin.'

The back field was edged with blackthorn bushes, a bountiful
source of sloes in their season; tight, hard marbles with a pale-blue,
dusty bloom revealing a black patina where your fingers rubbed.
Succulent they looked, but one bite and your mouth and cheeks
retracted and wrinkled as though a purse string had drawn them tight.
In the dresser in the dining room was a demi-john with a layer of sloes
in the bottom. Ritually, at intervals, this would be taken out by Dad,
the coral pink liquid vigorously shaken and the bottle restored to the
dark. We accepted such rites unquestionably and had no inkling that
the resulting brew was eventually to be poured into glasses and drunk.
Patrick's process was simpler. Littered about the back field were
empty jars which had once held potted meat or fish paste. These he
crammed with sloes. The jars were topped up with fluid by the most
natural method imaginable to a rising four-year-old, the lids screwed
on and the whole buried deep in the dark earth.

'When can we dig 'em up again?' Tim was never renowned for his
patience.

'A long time!'

'Not tomorrow?'

'No. Years and years. That's why it's called Slow Gin.'

The Brown family on first acquaintance seemed rather dull.
Certainly they were around in large numbers. The commonest was
the ubiquitous Meadow Brown. Now common was the right word
here. With their jerky, lazy flight and their large dark umber wings,
they resembled nothing so much as troupes of George Belcher's
charladies from *Punch*, addicted to flapping bombazine and bottles of
stout. But there is a gaiety about honest vulgarity which warms the
hearts of all but the veriest prude and we were never that. As in our
own kind, though not the birds we knew, we noticed that female
butterflies were usually the more colourfully attired. They are also
larger than the male, having several hundred eggs to carry around for
the first few days of their hatching. The female Meadow Brown has
patches of dull orange on her wings,, surrounding large black eyes

painted on the forewing, each enlivened by the little white dot that makes the eyes of Disney's animals sparkle so. Her sombre mate has smaller eye marks and no orange relief, or sometimes just a token. The eyes must have fooled the birds, for many specimens had forewings tattered around this position. A damaged wing is still quite useful for getting about with, whereas a damaged head spells disaster. It also guarantees freedom from the collector. All the Browns have these eye marks both on the upper and undersides of their wings, and appear to be watching you alertly even when the wings are folded at rest. The purpose of these sparkling eyes was easy to understand, especially when one knew that all these tricks were devised by God who also made Walt Disney. Now in later years, knowing that they all evolved by a series of lucky accidents and natural selection, the enormity of the chance becomes almost too much to tolerate. I think I was wiser then.

Preoccupation with male and female led naturally to familiarity with the little conventional symbols in the reference books. They also represented churches on the maps. Our village church was St Mary's, a female one with a tower which seemed quite logical. I assumed that churches with steeples, like St Clement's and St Paul's (well, a dome was a sort of steeple), were all given men's names. Finally Tim pointed out that the symbols weren't the same at all and my theory broke down. Much later in the Biochemistry block in Cambridge, I found that the Ladies' and Gents' doors were marked by these signs alone. This was fine except once a week when the History faculty borrowed the lecture theatre and squeals of dismay would testify to their unscientific bent.

I repeat, we never liked the word 'common'. In the books we found 'abundant'. This a grand word, with a good ring to it and it joined our collection of words that rolled off the tongue like 'middle-of-the-night' and 'back-axle' and 'Uxbridge' (our polite euphemism for a belch). Another abundant species, companion to the Meadow Brown, was the Small Heath, a pale tawny little fellow with a surprising turn of speed when alarmed. It must have several broods throughout the season, for the Small Heath is to be found from early spring right through until late summer. Many of the Browns, and others, do not appear until summer is well established, and this led to wistful scanning of illustrations, wondering if this or that butterfly would appear on the scene.

The first appearance of a new one was an exciting event, even though in most cases it was to become a familiar friend and prove to be abundant. This was especially so with the Peacock butterfly. She doesn't belong with the Browns, but the interruption will be excused. Beauty can be forgiven most things, and the Peacock (*Vanessa io* – even the dry, scientific name is beautiful) is one of the world's most lovely butterflies. She is also still found throughout the British Isles in fair numbers. Most years I have one or two on my Buddleia in my Yorkshire garden. The Peacock doesn't appear until well into July, and we longed to find one. Just behind the snowberries at the back of the garden, a dark, powerful butterfly rose suddenly from our feet. Tim reacted instantaneously and with a deft sweep caught it in the net, well above his head. 'It's a Peacock! I caught it in the air!' (this was much the most skilful way of doing it and we considered it rather sporting too). At last! With shouts of triumph we hurried to look at our first Peacock. To our disappointment it was not. What Tim had caught was a far greater prize, a splendid Dark Green Fritillary. I have it still, with its chestnut brown and shining silver undimmed by the years. But we were so disappointed that we had not caught a Peacock. It was as though we were seeking cairngorms and found a mere diamond.

Another peculiarity of butterflies caused a similar sort of temporary frustration. No doubt to ensure that the females are fertilized as soon as possible after emerging from their chrysalids, the males usually emerge before the females. Some of the Browns carry this to extremes. The male Meadow Brown is often on the wing some two or three weeks before his mate appears and the same happens with the next Brown we came across. This bright eyed Brown caused some difficulties. First was a practical one in that its favourite spot was the flower of the bramble in the hedgerow. Nothing presents a greater hazard to a butterfly net than brambles. Grasping thorns either hold back the net while the captive escapes or rip a long tear in the net. One option is to allow a shadow to fall on the butterfly, which usually makes it get up, and then catch it in the air, clear of blackberry bush. With a rare prize this can be an alarming risk. The safest technique is to place the net on top, holding it up by the end of the bag. The insect will probably fly upwards into the net rather than down into the bush. Once it has been transferred into a collecting box, the net can be carefully picked off the thorns. The other difficulty with this newcomer was that nobody seemed to agree about its name. Kirby called it the Large Heath. Others called it the Hedge Brown. The Large Heath, according to these, was what Kirby called the Marsh Ringlet. Indeed, this seemed much more like a large version of the Small Heath. I had called it a Small Meadow Brown, for that was what it looked like with its wings closed. Even the official surname was no help. Kirby said it was *Hipparchia* while others called it *Maniola*. Kirby was proving a dubious authority, and his remarks had a testy ring to them as though he knew he was in the wrong and wouldn't admit it. 'Of late years', he blusters, 'some authors have unfortunately transferred the name Large Heath to *C. typhon*, thereby causing unnecessary and regrettable confusion.' *C. typhon* was the Marsh Ringlet, which got our vote. Richard South, F.R.E.S., was our new champion, with three splendidly illustrated volumes. He called our butterfly the Gatekeeper and even Kirby agreed with that. So Gatekeeper it was to be. The females didn't arrive till a good three weeks after our first male and we had begun to despair of ever finding one. Each butterfly has its peculiar characteristics and the Gatekeeper has a perky impudence which is quite disarming. He couldn't care less what you call him.

The Wall Butterfly was one of the earliest in our collection, as it flies in May. The offspring of this brood hatch out again in August, so it appears twice on the seasonal stage. It is a companionable, friendly Brown, who loves strong sunshine and haystacks and hot, dusty roads and, of course, walls. That is how it got its name. The Wall has a habit of getting up from the road in front of you and flying ahead, say, fifteen yards or so. When you catch up to it, it moves on again. In this way it may stay with you for a quarter of a mile and then another Wall takes over with the same trick. We found them fonder of haystacks than walls but thought that to call a butterfly the Haystack would be a bit of a mouthful (though, on reflection, there was a little moth we had met called the Setaceous Hebrew Character – we looked up 'setaceous' and found it meant 'bristly' so we called him Esau for short).

The last Brown of the grassy lanes was a handsome, dark fellow, as big as the Meadow Brown – that is, about two inches across the wingtips – known as the Ringlet. I mentioned that all the Browns go in for the fashionable eye spots. The Ringlet almost makes too much of a good thing and sports a series of eyes and rings that must make any predatory bird wonder if it should have had that one for the road. Surrounded by rings of golden yellow, the black, highlighted eyes on the underside look very smart and give the wearer an air of gypsy devil-may-care. He is a stronger flier than the Meadow Brown and in flight looks almost black in comparison. There were three more of the Brown family we were yet to meet, but not that year and not in that part of Hertfordshire, so they will be introduced later on. *Satyridae* is the name the classicists gave to this bunch – the Satyrs. How such soberly clad frequenters of the lanes, banks and meadows, leaning to the dowdy rather than the debauched, earned the name of the orgiastic followers of Pan, I cannot imagine. From the Satyrs, however, it is a natural step to the Nymphs.

The *Nymphalidae* are much more happily named as a family, and embrace many of our best known and prettiest butterflies. Of these, the Small Tortoiseshell is the one that most people will recognize as it is to be found nearly everywhere in Britain. In town gardens and city squares it is equally at home as in the countryside. Small Tortoiseshells would hibernate in the Cottage, sitting on the ceiling beams in serried ranks. Warmth from the fires often would wake them in the depths of winter and they would flutter round the windows wasting precious energy. We would try and persuade them to feed on sugar and water, but the ones that woke usually died. A house seems an excellent place to spend the winter, but colder quarters are really much safer. We once found three hibernating in the middle of a field in a scarecrow's jacket pocket. I can't remember why we were bothering to search the scarecrow but no doubt we had compelling reasons at the time.

The Nymphs have a very sweet tooth. They are all strong fliers and must need a commensurate amount of the energy which nectar provides. All around us the fields were regularly rotated, growing sugar beet, turnips, wheat, barley, oats and peas and beans and also clover and lucerne. A clover field was a veritable honey-pot. As it was to be ploughed in eventually, though some was used for cattle fodder, the farmers were not worried by three small butterfly hunters treading on the crop as they would have been with wheat or barley. That is not to say that we never trespassed into the wheat fields. Once the standing corn was above your heads, you were totally hidden from view and could get lost for hours in the golden forest. We knew, however, it was against the code and besides, the butterflies kept to the

29

edges of the grain fields where weeds and flowers were more plentiful. So, there was little to tempt us in except the occasional Oak Eggar moth as he beat upwind on the scent of a virgin female.

The clover field was a different prospect altogether. The first thing you noticed was the noise. I wonder if Tennyson had been in a clover field when he penned 'the murmur of innumerable bees'? Only this wasn't so much a murmur as a full orchestra. Honey bees, humble bees, solitary bees, bees of all shapes and sizes all busily intent on their own affairs and humming and buzzing in every variety of tone and pitch. Put your ear against a telegraph pole on a windy day and you will get some idea of the noise of a clover field. We never knew which fields would be given over to clover, and we did the rounds each spring to find out, hoping a clover field would be near at hand. The first I remember was up the hill directly in front of the Cottage, beyond the Six Trees. These were six tall elms which stood in a row on the skyline, an indelible landmark of childhood which has, in all probability, fallen victim to the epidemic Dutch disease. Here in August we found the Peacocks, Red Admirals and Painted Ladies.

The Peacock is uniformly dark on the underside and at rest with the wings closed it presents a coal-black silhouette. On closer inspection this black is seen to be waved and patterned like watered taffeta, in no way as dull as it first appears. When the wings open suddenly the true glory is revealed of the four iridescent peacock eyes on a dark, rich, claret background. The effect is startling and no doubt intended to be so, for the butterfly will perform this trick several times when it is aware of you creeping up behind it. It is like the game of grandmother's footsteps. You freeze until the wings close and then move forward again cautiously. Peacocks also were our winter guests, sitting on the beams in pairs, still and inconspicuous until the early spring sunshine woke them to another year.

Close associate of the Peacock, the Red Admiral is an aristocrat. 'Admiral' is a corruption of 'admirable' and he is certainly that. He disdains any kind of fluttering but after a few strong wing beats he sails and swoops over the flowers with wings outspread. Only a broad band on each forewing and a band bordering the margin of each hindwing are vivid scarlet. These are set off to brilliant effect by a velvet-black background and white patches on the forewing tips. Mum caught our first Red Admiral in her hands. He was sitting on a fence post up the Tarry Road and we were all out for a walk. We had a habit of giving lanes and other local landmarks our own names, especially if something notable had happened there. Hence the Little Woods and the Strawberry Field and, on this occasion, the Tarry Road. It led uphill from the old water mill at the lower end of the village, and the first time we ever climbed it the tar had softened in the sun. Without warning the grey, dusty surface scab would slide underfoot, tipping you up and leaving a raw, sticky patch into which you fell. We arrived home like the tar-baby in *Uncle Remus* and the road bore the name in memory of the ferocious scrubbing in turps and carbolic which ensued. We were constantly being chastised for the vagaries of the natural world around us, it seemed to be part of the order of things.

Red Admirals have an aristocratic taste for tippling. They love fermenting fruit. There was an ancient pear tree next door and the fruit was rarely picked but would lie rotting on the lawn. The Red Admirals would gather in scores, uncoiling their watchspring tongues and thrusting them into the over-ripe fruit. They would finish up as drunk as lords and you could then pick them up, oblivious, in your fingers.

Rather more aloof than the Red Admiral, the Painted Lady is also less flamboyant. Painted Ladies are not always seen in large numbers, and in some years they are quite a rarity, depending on how many migrate from the Continent. The living butterfly has a pale, powdered, Louis XV appearance, especially in flight, which seems to disappear in set specimens. They are very lovely. I caught one in the middle of a clover field after some time spent in stalking her from behind, careful not to allow my shadow to fall on her, straining to keep her in view when she moved on (for once lose sight of a butterfly and it is rarely seen again) and inching up, heart in mouth, when she settled again. Slowly I extended the net – sudden movement would alarm her – until with one stroke I brought it swiftly down over butterfly, clover and all. Next, I had to hold the net erect to allow the captive to fly upwards into it. Then came the risky business of transferring it from net to glass-topped pill box. All this was successfully accomplished – by no means a safe assumption, for escape can happen at any stage if you are not alert. When I got home I found the collecting box was not in my bag. Disaster! The thought of the Painted Lady imprisoned alive in the box haunted me to distraction. On the sixth day I found her, still alive and seemingly no worse for the ordeal. I can still feel the joy of relief as I let her go, releasing myself, too, from a week of guilt and aching conscience.

A further benefit of the clover field was the absence of stinging nettles. For some reason the habitat discouraged them. A lurking patch of nettles would draw Patrick like the lodestone rock. He often managed to avoid the occasional cowclap and on good days would pass unscathed through mud and briar, but nettles were another matter and he would tread hesitantly in their vicinity. Sympathy was of the salt-in-the-wound type.

'Nettles can't sting this month.'

'That's got whiskers on it. They can sting me all right!'

'No, look!'

I had learned the trick of plucking a nettle by grasping it tightly and pulling it downwards through my hand. As long as you didn't push it upwards you only touched the underside of the leaves and didn't get stung. Even this scarcely reassured him. Mercifully the remedy was usually to hand and smarting knees and wrists were rubbed greasy green with dock leaves until the stung bits came up white like flea bumps and stopped hurting.

'Where there's a nettle there's always a dock!', I said pontifically. It was a sort of natural law. It had a rhythmic appeal, too, and launched us into one of our regular bouts of improvisation. This one went to the tune of 'Lillibulero' and was a good one for skipping downhill to on our tardy road home, a faster progress than jogging as you covered an enormous amount of ground.

'Where there's a hen there's always a cock!', carolled Patrick.

'Where there's a hole there's always a sock!', I joined.

'Where there's women there's always talk!', shouted Tim.

An uneasy rhyme, but we gave him full marks for observation.

Clover provided its own ambrosia in the days when sweets were in short supply. We would pinch out a tuft of petals and suck vigorously at the nectaries at their base. Dead nettles, the white archangels, were even better, though the bees had often got there first and the honey had gone. We spent much of the day munching and nibbling. Young hawthorn leaves were known by the village children as 'bread and cheese'. A turnip or sugar beet wiped clean of soil and excavated with the ever-ready penknife kept one busy for a good half-mile trudge. Ears of wheat, winnowed by rubbing in the palms and blowing the husks away, gave a chewy mouthful, succulent when green, hard and lasting when brown ripe. Late summer brought the red haws (bland like avocado), tart rosehips (which had to be seeded first for comfort), and velvety, young hazel nuts. Nuts on the ground always seemed undamaged but almost invariably proved to be empty or maggoty, discarded by the squirrels. We wondered how they knew.

Another family that soon supplied regular companions on our first expeditions was named, aptly, the Skippers. That, mind you, is the country name. The classical boffins called them *Hesperiidae*. They must have been running short of good labels, because Hesperus, the Evening Star, has no obvious links with the Skippers, who revel in bright, hot sunshine. And they do indeed skip. They almost hop from one flower to another. They are all rather little butterflies and anyone might be pardoned for thinking they are small moths. Of course, the distinction between butterflies and moths is not a very scientific one anyway. Butterflies are probably later models in the evolutionary timetable, and maybe the Skippers represent what used to be known as a 'missing link'. It is not always easy to tell moth from butterfly. All butterflies are daytime fliers but not all moths restrict their activities to dusk or night time. Most butterflies have the fashionable early Victorian waist, a sharp, narrow division between thorax and abdomen (some moths, however, are confusingly narrow waisted). Not so the Skippers, who are rather stout and hold their wings more or less horizontally when at rest, like delta-winged aircraft, as do the moths (or most of them). The other butterflies rest their wings vertically, held together like hands in prayer. The only sure test for the layman is to look at the antennae – the graceful 'feelers' projecting from the forehead of butterfly or moth. Moths' antennae come in all imaginable designs, from delicate combs to thin filaments, but those of the butterflies are knobbed at the end like the stamens of a flower. Even the Skippers conform to this.

For us, there were only sixty-eight species of British butterfly, so we soon knew their patterns by heart from hours spent poring over the illustrations. Anything we didn't recognize was bound to be a moth. The task, alas, is even easier today as the list is growing shorter.

The Large Skipper is so called because it is larger than all the other Skippers. All but one, at any rate. Even then, its wingspan measures only just over an inch. It is a bright tawny-orange colour, stocky with rather pointed wings and a vivacious frequenter of the clover and the flowers at the cornfield edge. A self-important little fellow, the Large

33

Skipper, and this pomposity is shared by the whole family to a lesser degree.

I must apologize, at this point, to purists among my readers for the unscientific descriptions of the insects in this book. There are many reference books which will supply accurate detail. For instance, you can find that the male Large Skipper 'has the hind margins of all the wings broadly reddish brown, and a large oblique black raised streak in the central area'. Or that the female is 'brown, with a series of fulvous spots beyond the middle on all the wings, and a fulvous patch on the disc of the forewings'. Good, heady stuff and there's lots more of it and it has its rightful place, but long before getting bogged down with 'five branched costal nervures' and 'hind tibiae with four spines' (all of which applies to the Skippers) you have turned to the picture to see what it looks like. None of our books ever told us about the distinctive personalities of the butterflies and moths. We found those facts out for ourselves as we become familiar with them, and I pass them on in case they may be helpful. Of course they may be dismissed as fanciful nonsense, but it was the nonsense of children which often contains a grain or two among the chaff.

It was through the Skippers that we became respectable members of the Established Church. One July day, in the course of a ramble with our homespun nets, we crossed through a gap in the hedge which skirted a clover field and came face to face with a real Butterfly Collector. The most conspicuous features of the stranger were a huge, professional dark green net and a clerical collar. The net, we later learned, was of the type known to the trade as a 'kite net'. The collar proclaimed him to be Dr Greenham, the rector of the parish. We were unaware of the stereotype, the mad butterfly-hunting parson, and I have never understood why the man with a net should be considered faintly ridiculous. Here was a candidate for awe and respect and this had nothing to do with the ecclesiastical trappings. He greeted us with the traditional and charming enquiry with which one butterfly man should greet another: 'Is anything on the wing today?' We felt we could trust him. One is often a bit cagey about these things. Our list was ordinary enough, finishing with Large Skipper and Small Skipper. 'And a Scarce Small Skipper', said Tim. This caused an interest that was more than politeness. Tim had been doing his homework and using his observation to good purpose. The Small Skipper was 'on the wing' in large numbers, a small edition of its larger cousin. The reputed Scarce Small Skipper was identical, it seemed, but it was not the first we had caught. Tim pointed out that the tips of the antennae of the Small were black on top and yellow or orange underneath. The Scarce, however, had tips to its antennae which were uniformly black, both above and below. If the Rector was surprised at such erudition in one so young (Tim was in his seventh year), he didn't show it, but he chatted with us about our favourite subject as though we were equals and we parted the best of friends.

The following Saturday evening the Rector came to call, and remained closeted with Dad in the dining room. After about an hour we were summoned. There on the oak table were two pewter tankards (this was interesting because Ethel had told us that parsons didn't drink beer) and a cork-lined box with about a dozen Skippers pinned into it. There was also a paraphernalia of forceps and hand lenses. Tim, it transpired, had been right. Only the Scarce Small Skipper was really called the Essex Skipper. W. E. Kirby's old-fashioned names again! Sure enough, the Rector had found that he, too, had several specimens which he had originally labelled as Smalls, and had caught one or two since he had met us. So the Essex Skipper was established in Hertfordshire, whereas its regular habitat was on the Essex coast. Tim was worried. 'It's still Scarce, though, isn't it?' We were reassured that although there were clearly quite a few of them around our vicinity, in the country as a whole it was a comparative rarity. It was what was termed 'local'. We had wondered what 'local' meant in the books, as it seemed to have nothing to do with the ales and stout context in which we were used to hearing the word. Honour was satisfied. It turned out that Dad and the Rector had been contemporaries at Cambridge. The Rector was a Kingsman and indeed, the living was in the gift of King's College. We eventually got to know this gentle, shy man very well and we and Ethel were sworn to secrecy about the beer because there were many people in the village who would have been deeply shocked by such libertarian behaviour in their shepherd. It was a revelation to us that grown-ups were not free to do exactly as they liked, and it was a strong but unspoken bond between us.

Strokes with a butterfly net are not as demanding as those with a cricket bat, but a certain amount of 'net practice' was essential, we felt. You needed a good eye and flexible wrists. When you caught your butterfly in the air, a sweep would bring it to the bottom of the net.

This was followed by a deft flick which brought the bag of the net over the rim, so sealing the opening. The old-fashioned nets were conical in shape, but this was a disadvantage. You were bound to get bits of straw or 'hardheads', as we called the cornflowers, grass seeds and other oddments accumulating in the net. This debris would inevitably finish up in the point of a conical net along with the butterfly, and delicate wings could be damaged and pollen rubbed off in the entanglement. The best nets were shaped like a capacious sack, rounded at the bottom to avoid corner pockets. The really dextrous stroke would take the butterfly neatly off a flower, leaving the flower behind undamaged. Of course, if you actually caught it in flight it was the equivalent of hitting a six, clean and satisfying.

Net practice was always conveniently provided by the familiar Cabbage Whites, as plentiful in the clover field as in the garden. They belong to the *Pieridae*, the family of the Whites and the Yellows. The Small White lays its eggs on our cabbages and the hatched larvae munch their way into the crisp heart leaves. The pale green caterpillar cannot be aware that by lying along the vein of the leaf it is practically invisible, to birds and gardeners alike, but after millions of years of trial and fatal error, the camouflage trick must have become an ingrained habit. The *Pieridae* are represented in Britain concurrently by some of the most common (the word can be used in both senses here) and some of the rarest of our butterflies. We used to watch – and perform with – the pierrot troupe at Filey in Yorkshire just prior to the war, where we were taken for our summer holidays by the sea. I thought the family name must be connected with the white pierrot costume with its black pom-poms for it is the same uniform worn by most of the Whites. It was a nice idea but probably just a coincidence. Nevertheless I still think of them as the Pierrots.

The Large White, the other garden pest, concentrates on the outer cabbage leaves and can wreak such havoc – at least its caterpillars can – as to reduce them to a filigree of skeletal veins and nothing else. Added to this, the larvae smell strongly. I have heard it described as bitter chocolate, but mixed with the bad cabbage smell it is repulsive. Even the birds won't touch them. The male butterfly is supposed to smell faintly of orris root, which is an improvement. If you stop growing cabbages and grow flowers instead (I did that this year) they attack your nasturtiums. Smelly pest the Large White might be, but forget its shortcomings and it is really a very handsome butterfly. Gramp used to tell us that if the dandelion had to be cosseted in a hothouse and kept moist and fed with blood like those ugly orchids, it would be considered the most beautiful and fragrant of blooms. It is something of the same case with the Cabbage Whites..

The female Large White is one of our largest butterflies, with a wingspan of nearly three inches. We found that in spite of their numbers it was very difficult to capture a perfect specimen. This may be because most of them are migrants from the Continent, especially early in the season. Ironically, though massed hordes may damage our sprouts and cabbages, very few of them survive our winter to emerge next year, and the spring brood is largely recruited from across the Channel. It's a pity they bother. The caterpillars are very prone to attack by an Ichneumon fly – a macabre little parasite which lays its eggs in the caterpillar. The grubs eat their host from the inside, skilfully avoiding any vital organs until they finally erupt all together through the skin and spin a mass of yellow floss cocoons around the dying caterpillar. This doesn't seem to make any difference to the number of Large Whites, but then it would not be in the Ichneumon's interests to do so. There are several different types of Ichneumon, each with its specific host. Great was the disappointment when a caterpillar of some prized species would be reared almost to maturity only to die when these ghouls made their escape. It brought us out in more shudders than ever Vincent Price could inspire.

To the long suffering vegetable gardener, any passing White must represent a potential threat, and the Green-Veined White, closely resembling and related to the Large and Small, often suffers for the crimes of its vandal cousins. It prefers, however, wild flowers like ladysmock and Jack-by-the-hedge for nourishing its brood. It smells of lemon verbena. I can no longer catch the scents of butterflies but our young noses were more sensitive in those days. The green 'veins' are painted on the underside of the hindwings and look as though the blades of grass where the butterfly likes to rest have stained their patterns on to it. A useful camouflage and another instance which makes random evolution look remarkably well thought out. This also seems to apply to another close cousin, the Orange Tip, where the green is not veined, but blotched and dappled on the hindwing, almost perfectly matching the patterns of the ladysmock and cow parsley flowers on which it tends to settle. The female is quiet and unassuming

37

with the pierrot black-and-white dress of most of the Whites. She is conscientious too, and stays mostly in the meadows and lanes where, like her veined cousin, she lays her eggs on ladysmock and hedge-garlic. Her better half has a taste for the flamboyant, sporting a vivid patch of bright orange on the outer half of the forewing. This makes him conspicuous as he flutters busily around the garden beds sampling stocks and other domestic *Cruciferae* whose flowers are related to those his lady is visiting in the fields nearby. The whole effect is remarkably jolly, like the outbreak of boating blazers on the river in the first warmth of spring.

The last of the *Pieridae* that we frequently encountered – last in this group, that is; it is often the first of the year to be seen – is a Yellow rather than a White and although not uncommon is always rather a special sight. This is the Brimstone Butterfly. The name conjures up images of hell-fire and Mrs Squeers, but it is the flowers-of-sulphur colour only that gives the name to the insect. I have heard it suggested that it was the colour of this particular butterfly that originally put the 'butter' in the name, and it's as good an explanation as any, though butter is not as yellow today as the theory would imply. But then buttercups are much yellower than modern butter, so maybe the old time butter was of a more brimstone hue. Our Brimstone is another Master of Disguise, and with the outstanding veins on the underside of his wings he looks exactly like a sere and yellowed leaf when at rest. His mate is a pale lime-green and even more leaf-like. Another dutiful lady, you don't often see her away from the buckthorn bushes where she lays her eggs, but the male is a frequent visitor to the sweets of the clover field. This is often the way with butterflies and moths and we accepted it as part of the right and natural order of things. The atmosphere of a clover field is not unlike that of a popular pub and it seemed right that the ladies should stay at home and cope with the children. That we were surrounded by Land Girls and the ATS at the searchlight made no difference. You didn't see them in the pubs either. What male chauvinist piglets we were!

Finally, another regular favourite we could depend on to appear in high summer was a shiny, metallic little character called the Small Copper. He is the last of his tribe in Britain, for the Large Copper had adapted itself to the Fenland and when the fens were drained, this beautiful butterfly became extinct. You may still see it, preserved in collections, but each specimen will be well over a hundred years old.

Rumour had it that it was still to be found in Wicken Fen in Cambridgeshire.

One Sunday afternoon there was a shout from Dad who was entertaining weekend visitors. 'Quick, James, there's a Large Copper on the village green!' I shot across the road with my net – never far from hand – and stared around, choking with excitement. Mr Berry the Constable was there with his bike, red faced, bulkily genial. 'You lost anything, young man?' 'I'm looking for a butterfly. A special one. It's called a L . . .' Tardily the penny dropped. Here, looming above me, was my Large Copper. Crossly I trudged back over the road, avoiding the eyes of the laughing row of adult faces at the dining room window. Some things are too sacred to joke about.

The Coppers are related to the Blues, and the Small Copper has the family streak of pugnacity developed to a high degree. He is as bright as a new penny and chooses to bask on flowers that grow tall and give him a feeling of 'Monarch-of-all-I-survey'. Any small butterfly rash enough to flutter nearby is driven away by an angry burnished little spark which then returns to its lofty perch. Any of the tall daisies and *Compositae* in your garden will attract the Small Copper, but the flowers it can't resist are those of mint. I always let my mint grow tall and bloom for this reason. A sunny day, and the mauve spikes are studded with glowing little butterflies, even in the Yorkshire Dales, not over populated with them.

These, then, were the members of the colourful *corps de ballet* which filled the stage from spring to late summer over the Hertfordshire farmland. The *premières danseuses* will appear later as befits solo performers. Other choruses, found in more specific habitats, lend their grace to the dance, but these stock members of the company were those we came to know best. Moths, too, had their place in our affections, but it would be confusing to introduce all the characters at once. Most of them will still be there, or their descendants will, wherever the hedge banks are still allowed to run riot in the chalky lanes and the scabious and knapweed and thistles can yet compete with the cereals at the edge of the cornfields. Some are struggling to maintain a foothold and a few have given up the contest with man altogether. *Sunt lacrimae rerum.*

CHAPTER THREE

Wartime London and the Country Cousins

Watkins and Doncaster in the Strand

I T was not until the war was well over that I became familiar with the traditional sights of London, usually by taking provincial friends round in a proprietorial manner. Keeping a quick eye open for signs, date-stones and notices, plaques and epitaphs, I could casually pretend that I was an expert on our impressive heritage. During the war, however, the sights of blitzed London that we would visit were little, personal shrines. Of course there were ephemeral shows, like the bomb which had fallen, unexploded, through Smithfield Market, just opposite Barts (St Bartholomew's Hospital). It had been defused and Dad and I went to look. In the roof, three or four storeys above, a wide jagged hole let in the sky. A hole indeed, repeated symmetrically in each floor vertically below and continuing through at our feet down to the cellar two floors underneath, like Alice's rabbit-hole. At the bottom on the rubble lay the ugly carapace of the bomb, immense, rust coloured and radiating evil (though I was assured it was harmless). Again, a section of terraced houses and shops had been sheared away one morning on the way to Paddington Green, amazingly leaving the right-hand wall umblemished like an open dolls' house, with patterned wallpaper, a clock and ornaments on the mantelpiece, hanging pictures and, I swear, the gas fire still burning. It must have happened a very short time before we attempted to drive by.

The large historic buildings and monuments were all hidden and inaccessible. Picadilly Circus, where I could remember the lost fairyland of kaleidoscope lights, Bovril and the giant Johnnie Walker whose legs strode briskly along for ever, was a sandbagged redoubt. Eros had gone (to Skipton Castle, we believed) and his plinth was a truncated pyramid of hoardings advertising 'Savings Stamps' and 'Wings for Victory' and Fougasse telling you that 'Careless Talk Costs Lives!' He was my second favourite to Ernest Shepard in *Punch*. Everything else seemed to be scaffolded, boarded up and 'Closed for the Duration', except the Zoo and Mr Churchill's Lion, and the sky was afloat with shoals of ponderous barrage balloons, glinting grey-silver when the sun shone. St Paul's was always there, though you couldn't see it as well from close to as you can now. One effect of the Blitz was the drastic clearance of the cluttering offices and warehouses which hemmed the cathedral in. So now you can stand back and really look at it – though at a terrible price. Our first imperative on a visit to Harley Street was to rush upstairs to a window to make sure the dome was still there. Somehow if that survived it seemed that everything else would.

Our favourite barrage balloon was anchored to its moorings on Broadcasting House. It was so near, we could make out the panelling on the silk and the quilted fins of the tail, so we felt it was guarding us as well. We saw one beside a cluster of anti-aircraft guns in Regent's Park, sagging half inflated on the ground like a stranded whale, and I felt something of the same helpless sadness that I feel today over these immense, pathetic castaways.

Patrick had a favourite illustrated book called *Johnny Balloon* which he took everywhere with him and left behind on a number eleven bus. He was inconsolable. It must have been a bus with eyes as we usually refused to travel on any other. I think it was *Picture Post* which had an advertisement featuring a large, staring eye. One of these posters on each panel on either side of the upper deck front windows gave the bus a surprisingly alert intelligence. Even more popular, however, were the few remaining ones where you actually came spiralling outside at the back to get upstairs. These were rare and Mum didn't like them, so access was problematical and an exciting treat. Another copy of *Johnny Balloon* was found and bought and Patrick was told the conductor had retrieved the original and brought it back to him. He was very pleased but quite unsurprised. People always did things for Patrick. He had a devastating charm though he was quite unaware of it. In later years whenever the family stayed at a hotel, Tim and I would dispatch Patrick on arrival to make friends first with the lift-man and then the head waiter. This gave us a mobility usually denied to unaccompanied children and ensured good helpings and even 'seconds' at table.

One of our sights still seems to survive. If you look at the bottom end of Trafalgar Square you will see two round pillars, one at each corner, each supporting a large lantern from HMS *Victory*. The one at the Strand corner has slits down it. These are, in reality, windows, and the pillar is 'The-Smallest-Police-Station-in-the-World'. On lucky occasions we even spotted a helmeted bobby inside using a telephone. I pointed this out to some friends only last summer.

In the middle of Parliament Square was a remarkable kiosk. At least, it was quite unremarkable until you got up close. Built like a gabled garden shed, dark green, its windows displayed newspapers and magazines, cigarettes, chocolates (this was curious because you couldn't get them) and the sort of bric-à-brac one would associate with a station bookstall which it rather resembled. It was only when you came right up to it that you realized that windows and contents were all meticulously *painted* – a sort of eccentric *trompe l'oeil* so beloved of the Dutch Masters (I learnt that bit much later). Why this elaborate deception, we couldn't fathom, but it smacked of the same mysterious strategy as the signposts and concrete tank-traps. Rumour had it there was an entire mock aerodrome some way from De Havillands which we passed regularly at Hatfield, built entirely of wood and canvas; hangars, barracks, dummy Spitfires, the lot. There were certainly decoy factories with painted 'windows' on the opposite side of the Great North Road. There was no door to our decoy bookstall but we thought it must be one of Mr Churchill's secret entrances to his underground offices. Perhaps it was. I never found out.

The tram tunnel is another vanished thrill. Starting from the Embankment by the railway bridge below Charing Cross, you could board a tram and, for about one penny, go rattling along underground like a ghost train at a breakneck pace all the way to Kingsway and the British Museum. The exhilarating clangour of it all! Trams were exciting enough. London trams didn't have overhead wire like Leeds or Bradford ones. We were a bit superior about this. In our book, such trams were mere 'Trolley Buses' and didn't really qualify for the title. But real trams which went both ways with the driver winding a horizontal tiller like the handle on the wash tub and underground too! There were a few stations en route, but most of it was madcap, clanking motion. They can never have filled it in. I wonder what happened to the tunnel?

My passion in life, which rivalled and certainly complemented butterflying, was the theatre. That would need a separate book altogether, but another vanished sight rose directly from it. That was Spaans, Wigmakers of Lisle Street. Think of all the glamour, the history, the excitement, the smells and the magic of every theatre from the first Globe to the final Barbican and distil them into one dark, musty, poky, pre-Dickensian little shop around the back of Leicester Square and you have Spaans the Wigmakers. Of course it was 'Auntie' Sheelagh who first took me there – we wanted some unobtainable green greasepaint as I was playing a witch at the time in a melodrama of my own – and she wickedly guessed that the place would haunt me for life. She deserved some of her own back in the haunting line, anyway. Our latest inspiration at the Cottage had been a ghost which

44

twitched your bedclothes off in the middle of the night. The floors in the Cottage bedrooms all sloped alarmingly – a sort of cemetery for dropped collar studs – and if your bed was at right angles to the slope, the covers would suddenly slide off when you rolled over. The culprit was gravity rather than ghosts.

Back to Spaans. As you grew accustomed to the gloom a packed conglomeration of masks and heads gradually emerged over walls and ceiling. Huge Bottom's heads, grinning skulls, cows, sheep, goats and devils, a vast gryphon and a pantomime giraffe like trophies in the study of some insane game hunter. I never saw old Mr Spaans come into the shop. I don't think he did. He materialized from the batswing shadows behind the counter and wheezed at you enquiringly, a deep, asthmatic orchestra. When I knew him better and was less shy I would politely ask if I could just look about. You stood still and simply rotated. There wasn't room to walk around. Before this I would many times buy an unnecessary stick of No. 5 or a tin of his own-formula nose putty merely to justify standing agape for ten minutes. Christmas time was best, for then you would have to queue, entranced, as prettily painted young ladies tripped out with bunches of spangled wands, or spears and halberds would be handed over the counter to be taken at the gallop for who knew what distant battles and impatiently stamping warriors?

Which brings me, by all too circuitous routes, to the one shop which made London worth the visit. Along the Strand, past Charing Cross Station and the London, Chatham and Dover Railway ('Is Your Journey Really Necessary?' it sternly asked), keeping on the right and heading towards Fleet Street (don't look for it now because the Strand has been widened and no doubt immeasurably improved and it has all gone), among furtive little shops where I was told you could buy luggage labels for your suitcase from any hotel in the world or where aspiring butlers could buy 'authentic' references on embossed and crested writing paper purporting to come from some of the highest houses in the land; there, if you raised your eyes, swung a grimy sign depicting a large Swallowtail Butterfly. For this was the long established home of Messrs Watkins and Doncaster, the Mecca of butterfly collectors the wide world over.

Anybody who is familiar with T. H. White's breathless description of Merlin's room in *The Sword in the Stone* can already picture the room behind the Swallowtail signboard, for it must have been based on this, the sanctum of Watkins and Doncaster, even to the 'real corkindrill hanging from the rafters which winked one eye in salutation'. It was also the most marvellous room that I had ever been in. I was nine on my first visit. Tim had been there once, about a week before, and had brought home some smart black-and-white pill boxes with glass tops and two display boxes. The ascent, and it was a long and steep one, started ordinarily enough, past a barber's shop, and you continued in a tightish spiral up old stairs with creaking treads and boldly lettered advertisements on the risers – a Victorian trick which seems to have passed out of favour in our publicity-hysterical age. It's probably the lift that has done it. You no longer need reading matter prominent at eye level when you pause to get your wind.

At the half-way mark, Tim saw that I was looking rather disappointed; as a result of his build-up I had hardly slept for excitement and this was not coming up to expectations.

'It gets better further up!'

Sure enough, round the next corner were cases on the wall. The Atlas, the largest butterfly in the world, was a bit of an anticlimax. Surely it should have a wingspan of at least a couple of feet! It was some seven inches across and hardly gaudy, but then it was 'Foreign' and of only passing interest. Eventually the summit and a glazed door; we were in. To something that was neither museum, library, laboratory, nor workshop, but with the character and smell of all these. Here was every butterfly and moth. In beautiful joiner-made old cabinets with bank upon bank of shallow drawers which slid open noiselessly and with sensual smoothness (for the slightest jar might damage a wing or snap off an antenna), smelling excitingly of camphor like Great Aunt Ethel, were all the illustrations brought if not exactly to life, at least to awesome reality. Here, under glass and grouped by family, were the Blues, the Browns, the Skippers. And mythical wonders like the Bath White and the large, handsome Black-Veined White, departed like the dodo and dinosaur. It came as an unexpected shock to me. I think I had really doubted the existence of many of them. Reality was something that only happened around one, like the famous Tree in the Quad. A jewel of a display case contained a collection of butterflies familiar enough but, incredibly, every one a miniature. Half-size Tortoiseshells and diminutive Meadow Browns. Occasionally things go askew in development due

46

to some rare, natural accident and insects hatch out with colour variations or deformities. Some collector must have spent a lifetime finding this caseful, for they never happen with any frequency.

Traffic noise from the Strand came up as a muted hum. Large tables filled the centre, piled with scattered papers fallen deciduously like last year's leaves all over their surface. And lost among these, surrounded by microscopes and setting boards, jars of pickled snakes and half-wrapped parcels, sat two gentlemen like a pair of elderly dons who rose politely as we went in. I say elderly, for this is how it comes back to me, but as a child – indeed, as an adolescent – one has little appreciation of the age of those you meet. Probably because it isn't that important. It is only when you begin to realize your own mortality that age becomes a yardstick of comparison. There were grown-ups and there were us. Or we.

Two elderly dons, then, in fading black coats and pinstripe trousers. These, of course, had to be Mr Watkins and Mr Doncaster. Which was which, like the Highly Respectable Gondolier, we could never make out and we were much too shy to ask. They were probably someone else anyway and that would have spoilt it.

Ever since Tim had told me of this enchanted emporium I had been surreptitiously making a shopping list. Had Dad realized what professional paraphernalia was demanded by our new craze he would probably never have taken the morning off. It was quite a list. On the other hand, it was an eminently practical one. Unlike fishing tackle, ninety-nine per cent of which is designed to lure and catch fishermen rather than fish, butterfly tackle has all evolved with an eye to the capture and preservation of the quarry. First were the nets. Real black fine netting with cane hoops and tubular Y pieces. I saved up for my grand kite net in later years, but these were great to start with. Also we got ingenious little folding nets made of tough steel strip. By twisting once into a figure eight and pushing, such a net folded neatly into a jacket pocket so one never needed to go unprepared. Mine was to accompany me to school, to church, to London – anywhere where the full-blown article would look incongruous or be frowned on. Then there were sets of glass-topped pill boxes which nestled into each other like the Russian dolls; four-inch ones for big prizes like Peacocks and Purple Emperors down to minute ones for Blues and Skippers. One to a box is the rule, for two could damage each other, to say nothing of one escaping while the other is introduced.

So much for the capture. A selection of setting boards is essential. The board must be broad enough to accommodate the wings and the groove the right width and depth for the body. You may have a large Hawk Moth with a five-inch wingspan and a body as thick as your thumb; there again, the Small Blue has a span of little more than half an inch and great delicacy is required. They still had a good stock of pre-war setting boards neatly covered with white paper. Wartime ones were just the cork without the paper. They looked ugly but really they were serviceable enough. Pins, for mounting the insect, came similarly in many varied sizes. Rustless pins with delicate heads, black or silver depending on the colour of the butterfly. Our large-headed pins from the sewing basket looked very clumsy and amateur in comparison to these slender ones and this was aesthetically a pleasing refinement. Setting instruments were not such a problem, for an ear, nose and throat surgeon (and by implication his sons) is rather well equipped for setting butterflies, with delicate probes and tweezers and the invaluable Spencer Wells forceps. These latter are for clamping blood vessels during surgery, but serve equally well to get a firm grip on a pinned specimen. Forceps which suddenly slip give a galvanic jerk which has ruined many a prize. I did get a marvellous pair of curved forceps, however, as aptly shaped to their task as an oyster knife or a shepherd's crook to theirs. There is a deep sense of pleasure in using the right instrument for the job it was nicely designed for – all the skill of our ancestors is in it.

The last items were printed name labels for all British species, to pin below the specimens in the collection, and locality labels which went on the mounting pin, underneath and out of sight, and recorded the date and where caught. Those we had not caught ourselves were to have a plain yellow label underneath. To put the icing on the top of the cake, Dad bought us one White Admiral and one Comma Butterfly, destined for our first yellow labels. These were reputed to be recently extinct and we were never likely to catch them. In this we were wrong, as I shall tell you later, but I mustn't be previous as they say in the Dales.

We left with our parcels and lots of 'Good luck' and 'Good hunting' and vows to come back as often as we could – which we did – and went to lunch with 'Uncle' Harold as Dad had an operating list in the afternoon. Harold Whyte was an eminent name in the medical world as he was landlord of the White Hart, bang outside St Barts. He later moved to the White Horse in Newburgh Street, near the Royal Ear, Nose and Throat Hospital in Golden Square. I thought his name and the colour of the animals which swung over his pubs must have a meaningful connection, but they were, no doubt, just coincidence. Barts wasn't much good for butterflies, though it had some monstrous, lazy goldfish in the fountain in the square. Some of the outer London hospitals had splendid gardens and kept our nets busy, but not Barts. But the grim old building has a special place in my affections. My parents met there. I was born there – though a respectable lapse of time separated the two incidents – which qualifies me as a true Cockney, a distinction of which I have always been inordinately proud probably because it cost me no effort in the attainment. The bells of Bow Church were sonorous at the time and were to stand unsullied for another six years or so before a bomb did its damnedest to put an end to Cockaigne for good. I later spent a little time in the bosom of Barts as a student.

The White Hart was a warm old tavern lined with dark mahogany. It had cubicles with dark red curtains and brass rings and smelt of good lunches and old port wine. 'Uncle' Harold was wide and genial with a wide mouth like Beaverbrook's and always a wide welcome for the Birdsall Boys. He gave me my first, gold-plated watch when I went away to school. It lies in the River Rawthey, if it has not long ago reached the Irish Sea, for one day I was photographing a dipper at its nest from a precarious hide, built on struts in the water, when the whole thing collapsed. I rescued my old plate camera, holding it high on its tripod like riflemen crossing rivers in Africa, but my treasured watch went to the bottom.

Harold was, I suspect, the original of the genial host in Richard Gordon's *Doctor in the House*, as far as any character in fiction is based on one individual person. Many of our adopted 'uncles' found their way into that hilarious – and quite unexaggerated – book. There was 'Uncle' George, professional bachelor, who had been left a handsome annuity by an aunt while he was a medical student. As this income was due to stop when he qualified, he was at great pains not to, the effort becoming increasingly difficult as time went by and his knowledge grew. His aunt was in time put wise to this (she hadn't died like Grimsdyke's Grannie) and stopped the grant until such time as he qualified. Whereupon he did so with flying colours. He had a beloved, huge old Rolls called the 'Queen Mary'. He and Dad took us to see *One*

Wild Oat at the Garrick once after the lights had come back to London. I felt that he would have been in no way out of place up there on the stage with Alfred Drayton and Robertson Hare. He slipped me a packet of Churchman No. 1. Afterwards he drove us round and round Picadilly Circus in the 'Queen Mary', as we lounged on the back seats with our feet up on the tops of the front ones, such was the space in the back. We had once tried to decipher instructions for doing some obscure alteration or fitting to the car. The leaflet said, 'First remove the rear-seat squabs'. We had no idea what 'squabs' were and decided it could only refer to the passengers. So all travellers in the back were known as squabs. As in 'Quiet you squabs, I'm trying to drive!' After the theatre we stayed with 'Uncle' George in his sumptuous flat in Mayfair with the pink sign of the Mirabelle winking away opposite all night. Tim and I smoked my Churchmen No. 1 and Patrick used George's electric razor. Not that he had acquired much of a beard in his ten years but experience is everything and this was a new one. When I got to Barts as a student, 'Uncle' George had become Dean of the Medical School. I never let on.

'Uncle' Cherry Kearton, who had lived with us in the London days, was the son of the great pioneer of big game photography. He was another Dalesman by descent, a close chum of Dad's at Christ's College. He was not a doctor. He told me he was an Insulting Engineer. He was enormously tall and when he came home in the evening he would throw his hat against the wall. Inexplicably it stuck and stayed there till he wanted it in the morning. He was also an extraordinarily accomplished burglar like Raffles. He had the knack of wandering around a crowded room, removing all the ornaments off the mantelpiece and pictures off the wall without anybody noticing until he drew attention to it. He used, it was reported, to strip Cambridge pubs bare like this and then amaze the establishment when he placed it all on the bar. He lost an eye during the war and would sport a black monocle. He had a glass eye for ordinary wear and a bloodshot one to match the morning after. Rumour had it he also kept one with crossed Union Jacks which he wore at parties. It is amazing that we grew up so balanced and sane surrounded from the start by so much delicious eccentricity.

'Uncle' Brian, another Cambridge friend, gave us our christening tankards and our teddy bears and brought Patrick into the world. He was in the Navy during the war and grew a piratical black beard which was rather alarming. 'Uncle' Brian gave me a fountain pen in 1945. We were all having lunch at the White Horse in Newburgh Street. He said it was the one used at the Peace Treaty in Japan. This was nonsense as there never was a peace treaty, it was Unconditional Surrender. The pen was enormously fat and black with Japanese characters on it and when you filled it, it used a bottle of ink in one go. I used it right up to my 'A' levels. They had just come in. It had been 'School Certificate' when I had taken that, but now it was 'O' and 'A' and 'A' and 'O' (*cum cantibus in choro*) like in the Christmas carol. I must have lost it after that but it was a comfortable pen to use. They used say that the new 'Biros' spoiled your handwriting. They had said that about fountain pens some time before. I'm sure relief nibs ruined your handwriting when quills went out of fashion. *Plus ça change!*

One delightful and I'm sure influential facet of our early life was our uncomplicated relationships with our parents' friends. We weren't exactly treated as equals, we would have hated that, but there was none of that *Pas devant les enfants!* The only grown-ups I ever disliked were the ones that talked down to us. If we kept quiet and fairly unobtrusive, they would chat away as if we weren't there and we listened, jumping like trout at words we didn't understand and usually getting the gist. Mind you, we heard a good many naughty stories that way. 'Uncle' Brian's grandmother had been a Gaiety Girl and married, like all good Gaiety Girls did, into the aristocracy. He had a very pretty and much younger sister who came home in floods of tears and great distress, having been accosted by an American GI on the steps of a cinema. Old Lady M. was stern. 'Don't make a fuss, child! If a man pesters you, you know what to do. Kick him in the balls and run like hell!' This kept us in fits of giggles for weeks.

Sometimes expressions were overheard which strained the imagination to surrealistic extent. One lady in the village served the resident battery as, not to put too fine a point on it, the local courtesan. The only one. I didn't know that then but I heard her described as 'walking about under a cloud'. I had intriguing visions of her going about with her own personal little black cloud floating a few feet above her head and raining on her and she with her umbrella up like the blackamoor in *Strewelpeter*. Once in Yorkshire I went in the car with Dad and Gramp to the Angel Inn in a nearby village. They were talking about the landlord, an old acquaintance. 'He's drinking himself to death', commented Gramp. This sounded full of dramatic possibility. Once ensconced in the porch with my lemonade, I gazed cheerfully indoors where they were talking to the doomed landlord. He was drinking. I was awatch, unwavering, as I didn't want to miss seeing him drop. I thought drinking yourself to death was a thing you could accomplish in an hour or so and that was what we had come to witness.

At Barts I met a negro for the first time. He was an African surgeon, tall and very distinguished and quite startling with his white coat, like a photograph in negative. We shook hands gravely and I was surprised to see the palms of his hands were pink. It is a sad reflection on our times that, although this stands out in my memory as the most natural encounter, forty-odd years later I am being anxiously careful as to how I phrase it. Little Black Sambo and Quibba and Quasha were old favourites of ours alongside Beatrix Potter and Pooh and *The Jungle Book* and yet silly people today try to read all sorts of demeaning motives into them. Mind you, Little Red Riding Hood was suspect in America during the McCarthy madness. 'Aunt' West, who needs a chapter to herself (a Barts Gold Medallist!), had been a missionary in the Belgian Congo. She had a precious Bible from those days with a picture of Jesus as a little boy in a garden with carpenter's tools and a halo. And he was a little black boy. And of course, we reflected, the Bible never said anything about his not being. It gave one to think.

Most of our adopted aunts were nursing friends from Mum's days at Barts and, as such, had prep-school nicknames. As well as 'Aunty' West, there were names like 'Aunty' Jert, 'Aunty' Bonzo, 'Aunty' Mike, 'Aunty' Trussie. Mum was an Edwards and the great aunts (bona-fide aunts of hers) would call her Hilda, on a rising scale like Lady Bracknell, but to nearly everyone else she was 'Teddie' until the day she died.

One spectacular sight of the grey, blitzed city stays imprinted on the retina of memory. It must have first appeared in the late summer of 1941. The air raids had stopped in the spring or thereabouts, and no street seemed to be without its gap or two, like missing teeth, with the familiar pile of dismal rubble behind hastily built walls and palings. Free dentures (like post-war building) have filled in the gaps and one no longer meets the old countrymen with grins of sparse tombstones whom we took for granted in our childhood. Miraculously, that summer, seeds which must have floated, barren, into London for centuries, found lodging and sustenance, and over the heaps and craters spread a coral-pink mist of rosebay willowherb. Every time I pull one of these persistent weeds out of my garden I feel a slight twinge of conscience for the time when I welcomed it with such delighted wonder. And with the willowherb came the Elephant Hawk Moths. The moth is beautiful, its colour matching the pinks and greens of the flower, but it is the caterpillar that feeds on the willowherb. Mostly on the leaves, but around teatime on a sunny day it climbs up high and nibbles the flowers as well. It is a handsome caterpillar, growing to some three and a half inches long with false, painted 'eyes', a front end tapering like a trunk to a tiny head and even painted 'tusks' on either side. At the back end it has the fashionable 'horn' which is worn by all the Hawk Moths. When its time is near to burrow and form a chrysalid, it becomes restless and wanders well away from the food-plant. This is when we would sometimes find them, hurrying along pavements or on fences or the trunks of the plane trees.

Such colour contrasts leave lasting pictures. It was probably about the same time that we came up to Skipton for a holiday with our grandparents. When we arrived after the long, grimy train journey, the table was set for tea. Wartime bread was tasty enough – and never on ration, except, briefly, after the war – but it was of a dull, wartime colour. Something like the granary bread of today but with a bit of khaki mixed in for good military measure. They never really knew what rationing was in the Yorkshire Dales. Grannie would kindly refuse our proffered emergency cards – extra 'points' on a piece of yellow card which came as a supplement to your ration book. Children's books were blue and adults' a dull brown like the bread and you had to bring your identity card as well. 'Nay, we don't need those up here!' The table, as I say, was set for tea. And the bread was white. Shiningly, dazzlingly, amazingly white! Grannie always made her own bread – 'baker's bread' was a term of some derision – and she still had a sack or two of white flour stored away. It is hard to imagine the whiteness of it, beyond the boasts of Persil (which was around then) or the extravagant claims of Daz (which wasn't) as it shone from the tea-table with a radiance that shouted at you.

Train journeys and holidays always involved the transportation of a certain amount of livestock. We never declared it. We loved the old Railway Guard from *Punch*: 'Stationmaster says, Mum, as cats is dogs and rabbits is dogs and so's parrots, but this 'ere tortoise is a insect so there ain't no charge for it.' Caterpillars would not look after themselves as the food-plant required changing daily and cages had to be regularly cleaned. Leave a pot of water for the plant in the breeding cage and caterpillars became suicidal and sorry, drowned corpses were the result. We could sometimes manage by putting a 'sleeve' on the hawthorn hedge in the garden. Hawthorn is a great favourite and probably provides a food-plant for more species than anything else. The sleeve was a broad tube of muslin, tied round the branch at the inner end and the twigs and leaves at the distal end, into which the caterpillars were placed, to graze safely on the living foliage. Most of our charges, however, had to be taken with us. You were discouraged from taking too much luggage during the war, even if your journey was 'really necessary'. This meant disposing of most of the caterpillars in perforated tins about one's person.

I think trains on the whole are much more pleasant today and you can enjoy the scenery as you never could. I cannot share the prevalent nostalgia for the glorious days of steam. You never saw much steam, though plenty of soot and smoke. Of course, I thrill to the existing myths, that pant pompously down the Worth Valley near my home today, with gleaming paintwork and lovingly buffed brass, but it was never like that. (I was once fishing with Gramp on the Aire next to the doomed Skipton-Carlisle line and I asked what 'L.M.S.' [London, Midland and Scottish] meant. 'Lamb and Mint Sauce', I was told gravely, and so I believed it to be for many a year.)

Steam trains to a rustic like me were by and large depressing, dirty and appallingly smelly. Carriages were redolent of damp soot with sad, dusty photographs of seaside resorts you were no longer allowed to visit, printed in various shades of H. P. Sauce. Look out of the windows – that is to say, peer out of the oval bit in the centre of the window which allowed you a view, about enough clear space for two eyes at once, the rest being coated in a sticky mesh to protect against blast – and if you weren't travelling through the nation's back yards, the countryside was scorched black either side of the track for a considerable margin much as highroads in medieval times, I had been told, were cleared a double bowshot to left and right. The only signs of life were licking little fires where hot cinders from the stack had found some remaining scrap of tinder not as yet reduced to ashes.

Shipley, that unavoidable junction just north-west of Bradford, was fairly typical of a small station in the latter years of the war. Travelling home for the holidays from prep school, we three and the other 'London boys' would be escorted to Shipley around half-past five in the morning to make London in good time. Trains would halt all the way down the route when there was a raid on in London, I suppose to prevent everyone piling up in St Pancras at once. The journey would take some twelve hours. Rain, leaking gas lamps and reeking crates which had held fish and retained the flavour. What glass still remained intact in the roof above the platform was painted dark blue to prevent the light that emanated from the gas from filtering up to enemy aircraft. There was no second class. It was either first or third like the Trinity Boat Club. Once on board, the darkness became an eerie twilight, lit by a few dim, blue bulbs. Hurrah for the hols! Our suitcases still smelt of gas and fish when we packed them for going back.

The human warmth on trains, however, was unlike anything encountered today. Crammed carriages of soldiers with here and there the blue of the RAF or the darker uniforms of the RN or the Marines. A few Free French sailors with pom-poms on their hats might be conspicuous but not, we felt, for their dignity. Our sailors had gone the same way as the police stations and had the legend 'HMS' on their hats, but no romantic name of their ship to excite the imaginative. Mostly soldiers. Soldiers who all wanted to show their conjuring tricks to small boys or their family photos to Mum. Snoring soldiers, soldiers eating, soldiers smoking Airmen and Woodbines, soldiers playing mouth organs. Almost without exception friendly and fun. I don't think Patrick ever sat on a train seat. He spent his entire travelling life on khaki knees. It was a great time for showing off your drawing. 'Squiggles' was an absorbing game. You drew a squiggle and passed it to someone else who had to make it into something. Faces were barred as they were too easy. The result and a new squiggle was passed back to you. The Association of Semi-Demented Poetry Hailers played Squiggles by post throughout our schooldays. There were eight Hailers, including us three; five boys and three girls, all Gilbert and Sullivan fanatics, and we sang 'Hail Poetry' from *Pirates* in parts when washing up. The squiggles adorned the back of the envelope. The boys were exiled in Yorkshire in term-time; the girls at a seminary in London's Queen's Gate area. Back and forth the same envelope would go, thick and heavy with economy labels, until there was not the tiniest room for any more squiggles. I wonder if any of these co-operative masterpieces still exist.

There is a very lovely, metallic-silver moth called a Buff-Tip. Its caterpillars feed on elm and are not uncommon in London. I had found a small colony of these and they were on their way north to school in my pocket. When small, the pale tawny caterpillars move up a leaf in a strangely decorative herringbone formation, the little black heads pointing symmetrically outwards. Regularly I would inspect all my charges on the journey, fussy as a mother hen and to as little purpose. The lid on the Buff-Tip tin must have been carelessly replaced. Standing wedged in a tightly packed carriage, with Mum and my brothers and soldiers and also a woman with a very small baby seated opposite me, I was aware of movement. The phalanx of little caterpillars had escaped from the tin in my pocket and was slowly climbing, with military precision, up the lapel of my jacket. Any moment hysteria would break out when the shrieking mother spotted the terrible threat to her child and the recriminations would be severe. Gulping with apprehension I pushed and jostled my way to the loo and there in front of the mirror retrieved the adventurers and restored them safely to the tin. A similar thing happened to me in the tube train later, with a baby grey squirrel. Sally, one of the Hailers, was in Holloway – the hospital, not the prison – and we were taking it to see her. Patrick did the same trick even later, with even more disturbing result. During an awkward interview with his C.O. in Cyprus, a pet chameleon scaled his shoulder from out of his pocket. The hypnotic movement of this lizard is weird enough anyway and in these circumstances the effect was remarkable, resulting in the extreme pallor of the interviewing officer. Patrick never told us what colour the chameleon went at the time.

On the few occasions when Dad could take time off to come with us to Yorkshire, we would travel by car. This must have been far more relaxing for Mum, but we really preferred the freedom and variety of the train. It took about three times longer then to travel the length of the Great North Road, even though there was hardly any traffic by today's standards. Petrol was scarce, and a familiar sight was the car with a captive balloon of grey silk flapping on the roof – it was actually running on gas. Night driving was hazardous as headlights were masked by black metal cowls which allowed a dim aura to reach the road immediately in front through angled slats like a meagre Venetian blind. We found the restricted movement in the car irksome, crammed in as we were, three in the back with the luggage, not appreciating how few children of our own age were then privileged to travel in one. Tim was interested and expert in current makes of cars and would assiduously check their number plates against the A.A. book to discover where they had come from.

Car games were encouraged, presumably because they kept us from squabbling. Squabbling squabs must vie with boilermaker's ear and galloping consumption for irritation value. The 'legs game' is fairly well known. Teams were divided into those who had a view out of the left side windows and those on the right. You spotted the pub names and counted the legs if any. Thus the Horse and Groom would score six, the Green Man only two and the Hope and Anchor none at all. Unspecified numbers, like the Spaniards were allowed to be two Spaniards only so scored four in that case. Arms were considered to be attached ultimately to legs, so the Queen's Arms, for instance, scored two. A Fox and Hounds was a good twelve points. We determined that when we grew up we would keep pubs and nobble the game with titles like the Six Jolly Centipedes or Ali Baba and the Forty Thieves All on Horseback. Tim had ambitions to be a tramp when he grew up so he would never stay in the same place long enough to keep a pub, but he was very generous with advice on names. I suppose Patrick and I just never grew up.

A magpie or a white horse (the living things, not pubs) would mean sixpence for the first to spot it. I would be rich nowadays but there were far fewer magpies about then. Some games, such as historical quizzes, were of the show-off type reserved for when there were visitors in the car. In later years, when 'austerity' was supposedly ended with the Festival of Britain, the Hailers would play the game of 'Country Cousins' on the top of a London bus. One of us was purporting to show the others round. 'And that's Cleopatra's Needle', the appointed guide would say in a loud voice, pointing as we rounded Trafalgar Square. Somebody was bound to lean over and correct us. 'Excuse me, but that was actually Nelson's Column.' Whereupon we would all hoot with laughter. I blush for us. When I was a student at Barts I spent an agonizing journey from London to our home in Sussex. A fellow medic and I used to attempt the *Times* crossword each on our separate journeys to Barts, then in collaboration over coffee in the morning. Sometimes we finished it. I'm better at it now but I think it has got easier. I was standing on a crowded train. Below me was a man with a girl on his knee. They were doing the crossword and making heavy weather of it. I could see at a glance they had got a long one wrong, right across the middle. I knew the right answer. Alter that and everything else would fall into place. I didn't tell them. I nearly did. I wrestled with my superior knowledge all the way to Haywards Heath where they got out and I only just won, but I hadn't been a Country Cousin for nothing.

CHAPTER FOUR

Woodland Glades
and Rides

White Admiral

A T the Cottage, minor jobs in the vegetable garden were detailed for the week, but we usually did these in a panic late on Friday afternoon. Otherwise our time was our own. Time for butterflying *per se* was reduced at the weekends when Dad was home. Then, though the nets were always to hand just in case, we were all on call for the serious business of logging. A morning spent working in the allotment was followed, with luck, by a lemonade in the porch of the White Lion and, after lunch, it was 'To the woods!' There were no men left to manage the woods – they had all joined up – so although we never felled any trees, in St John's Wood we were welcome to clear fallen ones and any dead branches lying about. This kept us in fuel for the winter, for coal was almost unobtainable for domestic use; it was needed by the railways, the power stations and the factories. We would go up by car (all the woods were on rises), drag out branches from the undergrowth, and saw and split the logs *in situ*. Small stuff made a grand bonfire where we roasted apples and spuds on hazel sticks. Logs were loaded into the boot and seats until there was no room for boys. Boys would then each trudge home pulling a long, trimmed branch behind him in a cloud of white dust. On arrival there was the car to be unloaded and the logs stacked to dry and our long ones to saw up.

On our own, less regimented, expeditions we went on foot. The lanes to the woods had high, steep banks and tall hedges of holly, maple and dogwood which sheltered their share of birds, animals, wildflowers, butterflies and moths. Apart from patches of bare chalk and the chalkpits, the land was mostly sticky, yellowish brick clay and flints. Walking along the edge of a ploughed field in moist weather you would grow steadily taller as the soles of your boots acquired a thickening of heavy clay. When the layer reached four inches or so you would begin to teeter dangerously on your ankles. Then you had patiently to scrape off the clay before continuing. Or you would impatiently try to kick it off which usually lost you your boot as well. Then things got even stickier. As more pasture land was ploughed up in the 'Dig for Victory' campaign to grow much needed wheat or sugar beet, more and more flints were brought to the surface. A newly ploughed field looked like a fruit cake covered in roast almonds. A familiar sight was a row of Land Girls in green pullovers and cord breeches, or, later, Italian prisoners-of-war in maroon boiler suits (siren suits we called them then) with coloured patches, moving with buckets up the fields picking the flints off the turned earth. It must have been backbreaking work.

The way to St John's Wood – our favourite one – was so full of beckoning interest at either side, it's a wonder we ever got there. Or back. You turned off the High Street between the Robin Hood and the Yew Tree into Totts Lane. The landlord of the Robin (who was also a Robin – small wonder I had my theory about publicans' names and their pubs) had built a wonderful air raid shelter in the garden behind. It was a deep, horizontal cave, shored and sandbagged, with electric light and seats and beds and stores of food. I would have moved in and lived there myself – it was far more exciting than a mere house. His eldest son was a fellow naturalist and a fellow chorister, a good sort. He also excelled at sport which I didn't but he was very nice about it. They kept hens. The hens used to get a sort of bran mash made with boiling water which smelt delicious. I never got to taste any but I used to come round often at teatime and have a good sniff.

On the opposite side was the forge and Mr Robinson, the blacksmith. More exciting smells. There was usually a carthorse being shod and Mr Robinson holding one vast hoof between his knees, bent double and paring away with a wicked knife, or pressing a red hot shoe which sizzled, first on the hoof where it left a smoking, charred imprint and then in the water tank. This was where the smell came in. Mr Robinson must have represented the intermediate stage when the smithies were evolving into garages. Many repair jobs on the few cars in the village were taken to him along with the carts and wains, our own included. He would listen taciturnly to the damage report, inspect bent axle or crumpled bumper bar, spit mightily on his anvil and rub it with his sleeve to clean it, and sketch out a diagram with a lump of chalk the size of a hen's egg fished from the recesses of his pocket. A great spot, the forge, in winter where you could always get warm and sometimes help to pump the bellows. Even in the summer we had to stop because outside stood a huge grindstone which you could wind with a crank and sharpen your penknife. Only a very foolish virgin would go to the woods with a blunt penknife.

At the bottom of Totts Lane it was past a little terrace of crumbling brick cottages where lived vast old Mrs Cox, always jolly, swathed in tents of black; black old boots and a little black hat perched on top, straight out of the drawings of Phil May. Then over the fence, this side of the searchlight, and into Wally Green's field. In the field was Wally

Green's goat. The field led to the River Beane where we sometimes went bathing before the water dried up, as it did each year (we then called it the 'Has-Beane'!), and emerged smelling of black mud and water mint. It occasionally boasted a speckled trout or two. It was also the haunt of Water Ermine moths and the bright black-and-yellow spotted caterpillars of the Mullein Shark. But first there was the goat. Wally Green's goat was tethered by an iron ring to a stout stake driven into the centre of his field. The rope allowed the goat to graze freely over a wide disc of turf which encompassed most of the field, cropping it like a golf green but leaving rather more divots. He discouraged any freedom of movement in others, however, and would vigorously attempt to butt all who came within reach. The solution was simple. By moving in a circle and keeping just out of reach, we would entice the choleric billy to wind himself tightly round his own pole. The field was then ours. This ritual would be calmly watched under long lashes by the other denizen of the field, a pretty little Jersey cow with the traditional harness on her face like the one on the Cow and Gate tins. We would always unwind the goat by the reverse manoeuvre before we departed unless we saw Wally coming when we felt explanations might prove tedious and scampered off hurriedly through the short cut to the bottom of the village green.

Wally Green was the village entrepreneur, buying and selling anything likely to make a few bob and, constantly red of face, he had the same unpredictable temper as his goat. He also had a white moustache, recalling Old Bill of the Bairnsfather cartoons, which hid his mouth like a Sealyham terrier. His over-riding claim to distinction in our eyes, steeped as we were in what the family called 'Manurial Rites', though the pun was lost on us, was his own special blend of fertilizer. He sold Dad a large sack of it in the White Lion.

'Best manure in 'Ertfordshire, Doctor! There's horseshit in 'er, Doctor. There's cowshit in 'er, Doctor. There's pigshit-in-er there's goatshit-in-er there's gooseshit-in-er there's henshit-in-er and, Doctor,' Wally worked up to the triumphant climax, 'there's batshit in 'er!'

Sure enough, the upper storeys of Wally Green's barn were festooned with generations of bats, resident since the days of bluff King Hal. Great bats, Long-eared bats and the little 'Flittermice', the country name for the Pipistrelle. The resulting guano was some four inches thick on the floor, accumulated over centuries, and used neat would produce the kind of scorched earth policy I have already described in connection with the railways.

Along the river bank early in the season and then again at the end of it, we would often catch the Holly Blue. It actually sits down on a sandy spit and drinks, the only butterfly we ever came across to do this. It has a slightly lilac tinge to the blue. The male has a narrow black border to his wings and the female a much broader one to hers and the underside is white, delicately powdered with blue. The effect is to make the butterfly flicker in flight like the old silent films. The Holly Blue sometimes came into the garden, though its real home was the woodland and the holly trees in the hedges. We would cross the River Beane at a shallow ford where there was a superfluous little bridge. The water rarely came high enough to wet your socks. Occasionally the river would flood and the bridge would stand out of a surrounding lake so you had to wade in to get on to it. There was a traditional legend about an irate motorist who asked a local farmhand how deep the water was before attempting the ford. On learning that it came just above the informant's ankles, he drove on, to find the water coming in over the sill of the driving window. Afterwards, it was explained by the farmhand that he himself had come through on his bicycle, putting his feet on the crossbar to keep his trouser legs dry.

Some way upstream, where the river ran through treeless meadow, we had a boat. In fact it was an old tin bath of a type still in use in most of the cottages, for bathrooms were largely unknown in the village. A plank had been lashed across the waist of the ship, supporting an oil drum either side. These acted to some degree as stabilizers. On a flood water we could sail merrily downstream for half a mile or so. The craft had to be towed, dragged and carried back upstream as it was too cumbersome to paddle against the current. One time Tim decided it was sinking and jumped for the bank. Patrick and I, pinned the other side of the crossboard, went in up to our necks as the stern went under and the bows rose up. We dripped and squelched our way home only to find the door locked. Ethel called out of the window that she was having a bath (a proper one) and we would have to dry out as best we could on the lawn until she had finished. We eventually got the boat out when the river dried up.

We were often locked out for one reason or another. Tim and Patrick had once been crossing the open slurry sewer in one of the farms. You could get across, as a risky short cut, by treading precariously on planks which bounced when you got to the middle, and you had to be sure to break step. Patrick of course fell in and Tim had to climb in to get him out. 'Auntie' Sheelagh and 'Uncle' Farquy were expected for the weekend. The stench of the returning pair was something solid. No way were they allowed into the house. They had to strip off and be hosed down on the lawn. Patrick's small black gym shoes hung festering on the wire, like Peter Rabbit's, for years afterwards.

Back to the woods. I said the route was full of distraction. Leaving the river at our backs, we would set off up the hill to St John's. The banks of the lane were a favourite hunting ground for two large, furry moth caterpillars. The Drinker moth caterpillar appeared from hibernation early in the season when about three inches long. It was usually the first quarry of the Easter holidays. It fed on the grasses and sunned itself. It liked a drop now and again, hence the name. Dewdrops mostly. It would spin a long parchment-like cocoon which matched the dried grasses to perfection; the moth would hatch out in July. The other caterpillar was that of the Lappet moth. A huge fellow this, five to six inches when full grown, found on the sloe bushes. At home they would feed quite happily in a sleeve on the apple tree, dark grey and hairy with fleshly 'lappets' near the head end which gave the name, and a beautiful dark blue between the extended segments when they moved. I must point out that these required careful searching. They were never easy to spot.

Up the hill there would be an old straw stack or two which always afforded diversion. You could burrow into the stack and then upwards, eventually climbing out at the top, black with dust. Then the parachute jump as you slid, exhilarating, down on to the soft stuff below. The first jump took tremendous courage – after that it was splendid fun. Ethel told me a pair of rustic lovers had shot themselves in a suicide pact in one of these stacks. They found their feet sticking out when they were discovered. I always inspected a stack thoroughly all round before burrowing in.

The last regular deviation from the path before the wood began was, in its season, the walnut tree leaning over the hedge of Foster's Farm. There was something compelling about these fruit that made an adventure of slicing in through the fleshy green to the immature nut beneath. Hands became stained, brown and indelible, but I could never resist them, like conkers. Fairytale princesses were always stained with walnut juice by their cruel stepmothers before being driven out from home, which lent the fruit a romantic ambience. I wish I could find a source of supply today as I love pickled walnuts. I still pick up conkers. I pretend it's for the children but that's only an excuse.

The final approach to St John's Wood was a rutted track with the oaks on one side and, on the other, a low scrub of sallow, buckthorn, blackthorn and spindle bushes separating the woods from the cornfields beyond. The sallow was a prolific source of pussy willow catkins in early spring and was know as 'palm' by the country folk through some association with Palm Sunday, or so I have always believed. I had visions of shouting 'Hosanna!' and waving tufted pussy willow branches, especially when they got their golden dusting of pollen. The early Christian missionaires had a favourite trick of latching on to local rites and supersititions and claiming them as their own, so the origins could go way back into the mists of woad and wizardry. A pretty, fast flying moth, the Orange Underwing, could be found on the palm early in the year though it often flew high above the reach of our nets. The spindle tree is a strangely mysterious shrub which is why, no doubt, the witches traditionally used it to tether their broomsticks. The twigs are square in cross-section and in autumn the leaves turn a bright puce. The pink fruits have four lobes and are rather square with bright orange seeds inside.

In the long grasses, feeding on the purple cornflowers, flew two more little Skippers here in May and June. The Grizzled Skipper conjures up the picture of a grey old seaman of the Ancient Mariner type. In fact he is a nifty little chap, dark sooty brown with squares of cream dotted about. The Dingy Skipper is a rather unkind name. We can't all be Beau Brummels. All the same, we had to admit that its dark brown dress was on the dull side. It is the most moth-like of the Skippers and always sits like a moth. Added to which, a genuine moth, the Mother Shipton (named after the famous prophetess of Knaresborough in her dropping well), grizzled, chequered and rather dingy, gave a very fair imitation of a Skipper in the same spot at the same time. Only the knobless antennae gave her away.

Among the scrub and scabious and meadowsweet sat, obsolescent, one of those defensive brick redoubts, built in chains over the South of England, a 'pill-box' waiting for the invasion. It was six-sided and squat with loophole slits all round opening inside to wedge-shaped sills to allow as wide an angle of rifle fire as possible. The door was always open and a visit often paid off with a sheltering moth or two and once a huge papier-mâché wasps' nest hanging from the flat concrete roof.

A strange wartime sight in the countryside in the early 'forties was officially, I believe, called 'Window', but we called it, simply, German paper. After a night's air battle, trees and telegraph wires, cornfields and meadows would be festooned with long strips of matt-black paper backed by bright silver foil. It was scattered from German planes in order to fool the radar and we later learnt that it was only effective when fluttering down. At the time, we thought it some sinister secret weapon to be dealt with. Hordes of urchins, ourselves included, roamed the district collecting balls of German paper, winding it up as we went. These balls accumulated like snowballs but were more durable. Some became quite enormous as the game became a competitive one. Try and get the local children to tidy up polythene bags and crisps packets today and see what response you get! Of course with so little packaging during the war there was hardly any litter to chuck about. Salvage collecting was a weekly task after church on Sundays. A pony trap, sans pony but with half a dozen children in the shafts, toured the village collecting everyone's waste paper. The salvage, as this was known, was stuffed into capacious sacks in a tumbledown half-timbered thatched cottage behind Kitchener's grocery. From there it was collected and eventually recycled to make more paper. And more salvage.

Butterfly bombs looked in no way, by any stretch of imagination, like butterflies and should not have been allowed to share the name. They did have a pair of ungainly wings (butterflies have two pairs), half cylinders on jointed struts which folded round the body of the bomb which was about the size and shape of a small treacle tin. These wings helped the bomb to glide down to earth. An A.R.P. chief brought a dead one to the village school to demonstrate yet another object we must never go near. There was quite a list which showed what horrible enemies we were up against. Some anti-personnel bombs looked like ordinary bean tins, the sort which invited a good kick in the gutter. Others looked like bottles. They even dropped toy balloons with poisoned mouthpieces. I never found any. But I never kicked anything suspicious either, especially tins. Balloons showed their intelligence was poor as we hadn't seen party balloons since before the war.

The entrance to the main ride of St John's was deep rutted by generations of long tumbrils drawn by teams of four or even six horses which hauled tree trunks down to Cannings' timber yard next to the White Lion where we would sometimes find the Hornet Clearwing moth. A very passable imitation of the Hornet but quite harmless. The car was always getting stuck here in the clay on logging work. Miss Cotton-Browne drove up here one day in her imposing fawn Rolls Royce with curtains at the windows and a uniformed chauffeur. He had a sort of leather dog collar round his neck. Tim said he was kept chained up at night. Miss Cotton-Browne was the last survivor of the Lords of the Manor. Things were still pretty feudal then in rural Herts. We had heard the story of the poor chauffeur who had once driven her home in a hurry from Stevenage. He had arranged to meet his sweetheart. The Stevenage road was one that took about eight miles to cover a four mile crow-flight, narrowly twisting and turning and doubling back on itself (Ethel would often cry after bath time that the parting in my hair looked like the Stevenage road and would assault it and brush it straight while I grumblingly submitted). At the gates to the manor Miss Cotton-Browne announced that twice on the journey he had almost reached twenty miles per hour and made the chauffeur go all the way back and do it again, slowly. This time the rear window opened and a gloved hand summoned Dad to the car. He was in his logging breeches and shirt sleeves and braces, swinging a bill hook. 'My man! Are you the Doctor's chauffeur?' asked Miss Cotton-Browne who didn't know him. 'Yes, Mum', said Dad, tugging his forelock. I mean it. He actually tugged his forelock. The serf! I can't report the rest of the conversation because we were rolling about in the undergrowth, hands tight over mouths, painfully trying not to blow the gaff by laughing out loud.

Miss Cotton-Browne owned the Little Woods, but not St John's. I vividly recall her visits to the village school. She was enormous and would sit on an alarmingly fragile chair in the middle of the room from which all the desks had been cleared against the walls and we would all show our paces with songs and recitations and things. When she tired of this she would scatter sweets – SWEETS! – and pennies all over the floor and we would dive and scramble and pummel each other for these prizes while she rippled hugely with chilly laughter like the wobbling mounds of frog spawn from the River Beane.

The main rides of St John's were in the form of a cross, intersecting in a big, central clearing. Smaller concentric rides crossed the main ones. Wherever a ride crossed there was a glade theatrically lit by the sunlight in contrast to the dappled shadows among the trees. In the glades in late summer, the large, shy dryads of the woods swooped and glided, the Silver Washed Fritillaries. Fritillaries are spotted. The flowers of the same name are spotted in the same way. We discovered the Latin word meant a dice box, appropriately enough, but such a mundane object to describe so lovely a family of butterflies. They all have a family penchant for bright orange brown, except the female Silver Washed who wears a delicate, greenish tawny, and are all spotted and blotched with black. It is on the underside that they show their individuality. The Silver Washed, largest of our Fritillaries, is mossy green on the underside of the hindwings, washed with streaks of burnished silver. Their favourite sweetshops were the mauve flower heads of the teazle where they were high up and alert for predators. But they were also to be found on over-ripe blackberries, with the accompanying hazards to the net that brambles always bring. They slept high in the oak trees and we once witnessed a breathtaking sight when the sun suddenly emerged on a dull day and brought glowing Fritillaries spiralling down into the clearing from the foliage above.

Another woodland beauty, the High Brown Fritillary, was less frequently met. He has metallic-silver spots on the underside and is difficult to distinguish from his close cousin, the Dark Green Fritillary, except that the latter lives in more open country. You never really knew which of these beautiful prizes you had caught until you had them safely in the pill box, out of the net, and could examine them closely.

The majestic Purple Emperor flew in St John's Wood within then living memory but although we looked for it meticulously, we never saw one. The iridescent purple males are said to have a liking for rotting carcases – about the only thing that brings them down from the tops of the oak trees – and we visited dead rabbits and stoats and carrion crows; we even sugared tree trunks with treacle, to no avail. I have met this mighty butterfly since, in another wood in another county, but I shan't tell you where.

Even on the warmest of summer days it can be cool and dank in a large wood and it was often welcome to make for the skirting paths where the distant landscape shimmered above the wheat and barley with the strange vibration that shows the day is really hot. As I have said, woodland butterflying is a natural paradox. Although the wood provides the habitat and the butterflies refuse to live anywhere else, you find them in the bits where the wood isn't. If you climb a tall tree so you can get your head above the canopy, you may well see many of them, high up, flying round the timber tops and feeding on the sticky honey-dew secreted on to the leaves by greenfly. But such a precarious environment is a frustrating one for the young collector. It is, in an apt phrase, strictly for the birds. And the butterflies.

For the wood edges you needed a long stick for your net. Not only were the trees and bushes fairly high, but the wood was moated round with a deep ditch full of meadowsweet and brambles and countless wild flowers, so there were difficulties in getting close. Here we would look out for one member of the most elusive, mysterious family of little butterflies, the Hairstreaks. The name derives from a jagged hairline streak of colour which characterizes the undersides of these butterflies. They are distant cousins of the Blues, but are much shyer and incredibly quick. You didn't find the Hairstreaks, they found you. All you could do was be in the right place at the right time. July and August was the right time for the Purple Hairstreak and the edge of St John's was the right place. Suddenly on an oak leaf a butterfly would appear from nowhere and open an inch-and-a-quarter span of purple satin wings which shone in the sunlight. Then, flip, it was gone – so fast you couldn't see how the trick was done. Here was none of the cat-like stalking and almost paralysing excitement which marked the capture of, say, the Silver Washed Fritillary. There was no time for thought. The reaction with the net had to be instantaneous for any success. Their speed must have taken quite a toll because it was only in the first week or so of their appearance, in late July, you were likely to capture an undamaged specimen. Right at the beginning of the summer holidays. After that some of them became unbelievably ragged.

A dour friend whom we usually met on these expeditions was Mr Fuller, the keeper, and his regular companions, an elderly liver-and-white springer spaniel called Lady and a more youthful, inquisitive black labrador who answered reluctantly to "Ere, Lie Down!' Lady was as gentle as 'Ere-Lie-Down was boisterous. The silver birch was, we knew, the Lady of the Woods – I think it was Tennyson – but the phrase for me still evokes the picture of a sad eyed spaniel I once knew. You wouldn't call her master a kindly man. It wasn't part of his solitary job. He was part of the woods like the pheasants and the hornbeam. Mr Fuller was always immaculately encased in faded brown leather. Leather boots, leather gaiters, leather on the knees of his breeches and at his elbows, those edible looking leather buttons on his tweed jacket, a leather pad below his right shoulder for the butt of his twelve-bore which he always carried, broken, over his arm, and a leather cartridge belt slung crosswise over his chest. His face was of taut, finely wrinkled brown leather with shrewd, pale eyes which looked beyond you into remote distances. He wore a crumpled trilby hat which he folded over the barbed wire under his crotch when he straddled a fence – a protective trick which I borrowed when I grew too tall to scramble underneath and still use today.

Dad came home from the White Lion once with a present from Mr Fuller. It was a large, flat tobacco tin, punctured with air holes. Inside lay a cabbage leaf and a Lime Hawk moth, resplendent in olive green and pinkish grey. The cabbage leaf was a typical touch. Most people think that moths and butterflies, let alone caterpillars, enjoy nothing more than a good munch on an old cabbage leaf – unless it be a segment of fur coat. It's the decimated gardens and wardrobes that give rise to the myth, of course, but it tended to be frustrating when we were anxiously trying to discover the right diet for an unidentified caterpillar, possibly brought by a friend or simply found away from the food-plant. 'Give it a bit of cabbage. It'll eat sure enough when it's hungry!' But of course it won't. There is no real reason, I'm sure, why a Small Tortoiseshell caterpillar, for instance, shouldn't thrive on cabbage or half a dozen other plants easily available, but what no doubt started as a mild preference has, over millions of years, become unvarying habit and unless you give him stinging nettle he will die obstinately of starvation whatever else you try to tempt him with. We kept to a formula, starting with hawthorn and dandelion leaves which between them must feed some hundreds of different species. If these were not palatable, we went through a further list but usually the reference books would provide the answer before hunger became acute. The Lime Hawk had laid a few hundred eggs in the tin – carefully cemented down – and these hatched in due time. The tiny caterpillars were transferred with a paint brush to a lime leaf and about a dozen of them were eventually reared to maturity the following spring.

The popular success of his gift kindled a flame in Mr Fuller and on occasions when we met he would wordlessly slip us a Swan Vestas matchbox. We had been warned that this might happen and to thank him politely whatever the contribution. The box would be crammed with butterflies and moths, all alive and kicking – how he caught them we couldn't guess – mostly Meadow Browns and common species but the occasional Fritillary or other scarcity, and all quite ruined. Sadly, out of his sight, we would release them, their pollen rubbed off, their beauty marred, never having the courage to explain it to him. We realized in our way that beneath the gnarled, leather exterior of our taciturn friend the keeper, albeit stern executioner, was a soul that could be hurt like the insects he gave us.

Mr Fuller was a strict gamekeeper but certainly not a sadistic one. His victims were the predators of the pheasants and partridges and their chicks and the moral issues of the sentimentalists had no place in his creed. Rats, weasels and stoats, carrion crows and grey squirrels fell to his unerring shotgun, but he was selective. He would shoot the vixen but leave the greying dog fox who was getting slow and could cull only the sick birds who couldn't escape or the last, elderly member of the covey to leave the ground. We never met the keeper of the woods over at Ardeley, a pretty, thatched village some way off our beaten track, but we saw proof of his handiwork. Once on the edge of these woods I saw a dead partridge on the ground, the breast rawly gaping. A fox? I bent to examine it. Dad's stick prodded quickly down on the bird and hidden iron jaws snapped shut where a second later my hand would have been. He said nothing. The lesson needed no elaboration. The returning fox would have been caught by the muzzle. If traps were inspected daily the beasts would be spared too much suffering, but a dead ermine we found trapped here had eaten its own hind leg down to clean bone in the attempt to escape. In the wood itself was the macabre spectacle of the gamekeeper's larder. Hung by their necks in forked twigs of the hazel bushes were the customary crows, jays and magpies, and skins of foxes, badgers and stoats were nailed to the sides of a wooden hut. But there were other corpses which struck horror into us. Tawny owls and barn owls and huge long-eared owls rotted there, and sparrow hawks and even a green woodpecker. What possible threat to game could be held against the woodpecker, we could not conceive. We released a live squirrel from a gin – not without considerable danger to ourselves as he naturally fought viciously as we tried to help him. Of course, we had no business to be there at all.

Part of St John's Wood we christened the Strawberry Field because it was our most plentiful source of wild strawberries which we picked for jam and pies or more often simply ate by the handful on the spot. Later in the year at blackberrying time it would yield the even more succulent dewberries, low growing large blackberries with a powdery bloom like a grape. And no prickles. They were found low down under thorny scrub which was completely uncontrolled and hard to penetrate. Here we would find the larder of the red backed shrike, a miniature of the keeper's gibbet, with beetles, bumble bees and small mice impaled on the blackthorn spikes. The big grassy nests of dormice were hidden here too. The wide-eyed adults would come out and clamber crossly about, fluffy ginger balls of indignation. The miniscule harvest mice were quite common, nesting in the cornfields or feeding on the ripe ears. There were also harvest men, long thin-legged spiders with small spherical bodies, and harvest mites, tiny red spiders that bit and made an itch. They had red blood like ours.

The Strawberry Field was a favourite haunt of the Burnet moths, or 'Buzzy-bee moths' as Patrick christened them. These rather elongated little moths have a burnished bottle-green forewing, decorated with crimson spots, and a crimson hindwing. There is a Five-spot Burnet and a Six-spot Burnet. Conveniently they appear at slightly different times of the year, so sparing us (and presumably themselves) undue confusion. Sometimes the air would be full of them, lazily buzzing about. The Strawberry Field was desecrated not long after the war. This prolific sanctuary was dragged out by the roots with tractors, cleared with bulldozers and ploughed up for yet more arable land.

The way to the Little Woods lay across the brickfields. There must have been a brickworks and kilns there at some time where the local building material had been made, an mellow orange brick in conjunction with old oak timbers turned silvery by the sun. The huge conical chimney and inglenook in the Cottage were built of such brick. No trace of the brickworks remained to our untutored eyes but the name was still there. There was a splendid pond, however, where we used to fish for carp. It was filled with toad spawn every spring, not in large quivering clumps like frog spawn, but long spotted filaments which crossed and recrossed the pond like gelatinous spaghetti. The Little Woods were partly very young fir plantation and partly low scrub with sallows and dogwood and thorn. There was also quite a lot of gorse and broom. This was a haunt of the Green Hairstreak, rather smaller than its purple cousin, but just as nippy. We never found many. Any Hairstreak in the net made the day a good one. It may be there were more about than we realized. The Green Hairstreak is green on the underside only. The upperside is a dark grey-brown and rather nondescript. The butterfly was on the wing in May and came on again in August when the Purple were flying as well. Green seems an ideal colour for camouflage and it is surprising that only the Green Hairstreak really sports it. I don't count the few Fritillaries that have small patches of green among the rest, and the female Brimstone is a very subdued green. Plenty of moths favour green but not butterflies. There is quite a large family of Emerald moths. They fly mostly at night which seems rather a waste.

The keeper in the Little Woods was distinctly unfriendly and once when we were assailing a hawthorn tree after a magpie's roofed nest he took our names and swore he was going to prosecute us for trespass like the notice said. We were always at it. 'Forgive us our trespasses' had a specially sincere ring every night. We assured him that you could only be summonsed for trespass if you were proved to be doing wilful damage. And if we doing any damage it certainly wasn't wilful. All of which was perfectly true but it must be disconcerting to be informed of the fact, in unison, by three small boys ranging from six to ten years, their heights descending in steps like the Ovaltine picture. We had been careful to learn it by heart in case it came in useful. We never saw much of him after that, only in the distance, and he certainly never bothered us again. Of course it was in the Little Woods that Tim first caught the Cinnabar and it all began. It was an unparalleled wood for nightingales. I must confess to finding a robin's song as lovely though with less inventiveness, but the nightingale has the inspiration to sing at night. Like the sultans of old in the *Arabian Nights*, we would hear them from the bedroom windows in the stillness, a score of nightingales over a mile away singing in the dark in the Little Woods.

★

High Wood was just that, with tall trees where the sparrow hawks nested, and carrion crows. Here was a good deal of small elm, too, among the other woodland scrub and bushes, and far more exposed chalk than in the other woods. Edible mushrooms such as the wood blewits and parasols grew here, delicious in stews or with bacon (Tiger bacon we called it in the war – it was yellow and black and stripey) and also the two really poisonous ones. Nobody would eat the fly agaric – it is the Disney one, red with white spots and obviously looks poisonous, though slugs love it. The dangerous one is the death cap which looks a bit like a field mushroom. But you can't peel it and, unmistakable give-away, it has a hollow stem. On one occasion in 1943 we returned from High Wood with two huge baskets of assorted mushrooms. Great Aunt Ella was temporarily in charge at the Cottage in our parents' absence and we smugly anticipated congratulations and expressions of delight. To our consternation she would not take the responsibility of trusting our field knowledge and made us throw them away as they might be dangerous. We were scandalized by such wanton waste of food and hid them in the garden pending Dad's return. He, of course, vindicated our selection but, by the time he inspected them, the mushrooms had become soggy and unpalatable. Mum explained tactfully that not everyone could be expected to trust in the harmlessness of apparent toadstools on the assurance of small boys, and Aunt Ella magnanimously made us a handsome (and quite unnecessary) apology. More than that, she offered to accompany us on the next forage.

To our surprise she came with us when we replenished the baskets from the same source and thoroughly enjoyed the proceeds at the following Sunday lunch. On reflection she probably checked them thoroughly with Dad before risking it, but honour was satisfied and we looked on her with an awakened respect. She had revealed an unsuspected knowledge of natural history and had proved to be an expert on wild flowers far beyond our limited experience. She (and Mr Churchill who was born on the same day) was almost exactly sixty years older than I to the day. This would have made her sixty-nine on the mushrooming trip. What the expedition had cost her in aches and pains we never guessed, but she didn't venture out with us again despite our pleading. Thereafter we would bring unfamiliar plants back to her for identification whenever she came to stay and I would send her sketches for similar information when she was at her home in

Eastbourne. Her own flower drawings were exquisite. Sadly, I fear, not one survives.

There were long, gloomy rides in much of High Wood, with here and there, for keepers, I suppose, a pump like we had on the village green and nesting boxes and food troughs for the pheasants. Empty now were wooden sheds on metal wheels like old bathing machines where the underkeepers used to live all summer to protect the young birds before they themselves were called up to protect the rest of us. The High Wood prima donna was the White Letter Hairstreak. Not immediately noticeable for its glamour, and yet as dainty a little butterfly as any, the White Letter Hairstreak is a plain grey-brown on the upperside. The hindwings have a well defined pair of little tails, tipped with white. Both Green and Purple have suspicions of tails, but these are unmistakable. The underside is a lighter, warmer brown and the white streak finishes at the bottom in a bold 'W', the eponymous white letter. Below at the base is a fiery orange zig-zag, as though a plain but expensive gown were relieved by a thin string of pearls and a single jewel. Again, not always met with, it was a prize catch on the elms in July. If this species survived until the arrival of Dutch elm disease, I fear for its safety now.

Box Wood, the last of our local woods within easy walking distance, was at first nothing special. It had a certain amount of beech which is good for bluebells but nothing much else except fungi as the beech hogs all the light. We did go there once in winter, on a telephoned request for Dad, who was known locally for his bird lore, to go and identify a possible siskin. Only one, which seemed unlikely as these finches spend the winter in little flocks. It proved to be a robin – indubitably by its pose and behaviour – but a perfect albino, as though carved out of living ivory.

One day in 1942 the buzz went round that Commas has been seen in Box Wood and, a little later, a White Admiral. These were the two we had bought at Watkins and Doncaster knowing how unlikely it was we would ever see them. In fact they had neither of them become extinct, but the Comma was restricted to Gloucester and Hereford and the White Admiral to a small area of the New Forest. Why they both extended their range so suddenly and dramatically, I cannot surmise, but their appearance brought tremendous excitement with it. I couldn't wait to get to Box Wood. Dr Greenham had been and had caught a Comma thinking (in flight) it was a Fritillary. I must have been favoured by the gods for I saw five before I even entered the wood. As luck would have it there was a clover field right next to the southern edge of the wood and there in the May sunshine I found them. Even Mum had been infected by our agitation and had come along. She never let me forget the event. I must admit that our Mother does not figure largely in the expeditions and the reason is a sad one. Early in the war she became a victim of severe chronic arthritis which lasted for the rest of her life. She had to cope with three children, often in excruciating pain, but as she was the first to point out, had she not had to keep moving she could have lost the power of movement altogether.

The Comma day must have been a good day. I know it was a warm, sunny afternoon, I can still see every detail. The Comma butterfly deserves a little description. It is one of the Nymphs of the *Vanessa* family along with the Peacocks and the Tortoiseshells, but it has some unique qualities. First, it is deeply scalloped and indented on the borders of its wings like the outline of the map of Norway. These stylized tatters give a convincing dead leaf effect. Secondly, when hibernating, no doubt with regard to that, it scorns shelter of any kind but, a true spartan, sits on a bare branch among snow, tempest or flood, and simply waits for spring. It is bright ginger-brown on the upperside, marked with black, and varying from very dark umber to ochre on the underside with a grain like a walnut cabinet. On the underside of the hindwing there is a conspicuous white 'comma'. The Latin name is *c-album*. In fact it is a 'c' on the port side and a comma on the starboard. Commas are skilful fliers beyond the ordinary, indulging in swift aerobatics – fast wing beats followed by swooping glides and rolls which make them very hard to catch. I was in a high fever of excitement and these impudent butterflies treated me to the sort of baiting meted out by Kipling's Armadilloes to Painted Jaguar. They flew round me every which way, darted off to the maples in the thicket edge, settled on my head, perched on the rim of my net and laughed at me. My family laughed at me. As Gramp would have said, 'Ee! They hadn't laffed so much since t'closet froze!' My antics must have been grotesque. In the end, Dad caught one and I caught two. A memorable day. Since then the Comma has become quite abundant over the years in all the southern counties and has even left the woods for gardens where you may see it on buddleia in the late summer, for it has a second annual brood. But like the Armadilloes they are not so clever nor so cheeky as they were in the High and Far Off Times.

The White Admirals colonized Box Wood in June of that remarkable year. Flying in the restricted spaces of woodland must call for considerable expertise, and these are the most superbly graceful of all butterflies in the air. Like its *Vanessa* cousin, the Red Admiral, which has sparse though vivid red, the White Admiral is mainly brownish black on the upperside. Just a curved band of white on each border justifies its name. The underside is much prettier, being a golden brown with the same white band showing through, and powder blue near the body. In flight as it flaps and glides and curvets among the foliage, the double effect merges perfectly with dappled shadow and the oval sun spots dancing on the leaves. Always a difficult prize to catch – it was a great bramble flower addict in addition to its aeronautical skill – the White Admiral extended its range to most of the southern woods and with its quiet beauty and its elegant flight it will always epitomize for me the English woodland. Why, with the Comma, it should have quickly become so widespread, I don't think even the experts understand, and there may be hope for those butterflies whose numbers are dwindling alarmingly today, providing we can still offer them the habitats in which to expand.

CHAPTER FIVE

Village Wildlife and Downland Beauties

The Grayling

CARP fishing in the brickfields pond involved a technique of our own invention which would certainly never appeal to the purists, but then there was none of that appalling litter such as nylon cast (indeed, it hadn't been invented) and discarded barbed hooks and lead shot which cause cruel havoc and toxic disease among the bottom-feeding waterfowl today. Our tackle consisted of a brick, a good length of old washing line and a bucket. The brick was tied securely to the end of the rope and hurled into the middle of the pond. We then hauled it back, bringing with it a tangled mass of waterweed. Enmeshed in the weed were the flapping carp, two to four inches in length, which were transferred to the water in the bucket. All sorts of other pond life would emerge as well. Dragonfly nymphs abounded as did the flying adults above the water – large long-bodied 'Devil's darning needles' which can actually fly backwards, some with tinted wings; big flat-bodied blue ones, and swarms of little black and blue, black and green and black and brown banded demoiselles. The great diving beetle and the silver diving beetle and their vicious larvae were prevalent and scores of water boatmen, pond skaters, whirligigs, caddises and other teeming occupants of the pond. The weed was thrown back when we had transferred our catch and the brick sent in again.

We never got into dragonflies much, apart from reckoning there were over a dozen species, most of them common enough. The reason was that they had such discouraging long Latin names. The huge, faceted eyes of the larger dragonflies are remarkably beautiful, the brittle wings with their gothic lattice of veins and the striking patterns of the body, and then you find it is known as *Aeschna cyanea* Müll or some such, which is enough to turn anyone off. People should be more imaginative about names. I once knew a girl called Madeleine Wrigley and of course she was known everywhere as 'Wriggling Madly'. I have an eccentric basset called Belinda. A good, sensible name for a dog though it is the only sensible thing about her. However, we fostered another basset for some months and her name was Mercy. Now bassets are forever getting lost – quite deliberately – and need regular recalling. Shouting 'Belinda!' is harmless enough. Wayfarers assume rightly that either your dog or your wife has managed temporarily to lose you. But the effect of a poor fellow shouting 'Mercy! Mercy!' from behind a dry-stone wall is disconcerting, to say the least.

The carp were not destined for some ritual kosher feast, but for an indolent life in one of the aquaria of 'Uncle' Len. We also supplied him with newts for another tank. These came from a different pond and the tackle was a little more sophisticated, involving black cotton on canes and bent pins baited with small earthworms. We found the common newt and the magnificent great crested newt with his bright orange tummy and erect dorsal crest over the body and tail. The rainbow colours of the males in the breeding season were agressively decorative. Patrick still retains an absorbing interest in aquaria.

'Uncle' Len would welcome the additions to his family by singing a naughty music hall song entitled. 'Has anybody seen my Tiddler?' He was a redoubtable East Ender who had retired from London to rural Herts to be out of the way of the bombing, and probably the most courageous man I ever knew. It was certainly not fear for himself that drove him out of London, more a concern for his family who had to desert him every time they went to the Underground, the communal air-raid shelter used by a large majority of Londoners. The stations were a maze of bunk beds whenever we went down there, many little blocks partitioned off with blankets like Bedouin tents, the permanent residences of families who very probably had nowhere left above ground. For 'Uncle' Len it was either staying put or living down there for he had contracted spondulitis, the disease where the vertebrae become fused together making the spine totally inflexible. He had the choice of what position he would gradually 'set' in. As he was well taller than average, an upright stance would have posed problems and a sitting position would have been far too restrictive. So 'Uncle' Len stood with his head and shoulders thrust forward, still able to walk at a shuffle, his weight resting on his two sticks, Tom and Dick. Dick was the one with the varicose veins.

'Uncle' Len's eyes were slightly protuberant, a symptom of the disease, and with his black hair and heavy black eyebrows he was strongly reminiscent of George Robey whom he often imitated with consummate artistry. 'Nobody in sight!' I never saw the Prime Minister of Mirth on stage, but I felt I knew his routines as if I had. An even greater facial likeness to 'Uncle' Len was the great French actor, Fernandel. They could have been twins. 'Uncle' Len had been on the 'Halls' at one stage of his career, and played the big steel banjo, a skill he had picked up as a nipper in a barber's shop down the Mile End Road. But then he had done most things. He had been failed as a lorry driver in the Great War because of his flat feet, so slogged round for four years in the infantry which only insisted on feet.

He lived with his wife, 'Auntie' Ethel, in a little, semi-detached brick cottage at the bottom of the High Street. There was an ironwork gate which he would never oil because it was better than a doorbell. He half lay, half sat in a tilted chair, back to the lace curtained window with a mirror on the wall opposite so he could immediately see who was coming whenever the gate complained. Traditionally we would stop at the gate and whistle the corny phrase from the 'Policeman's Holiday', to which he would whistle in reply. Later we obtained a second-hand dentist's chair (the chair, not the dentist, he would insist) from a friend in Wimpole Street where the dentists all lived and we fancied we could see them staring sadistically out of the windows and rubbing their hands together in gleeful anticipation of the next patient. This chair was ideal, as of course he slept in it as well and the angle could be adjusted. He never went upstairs in his cottage in his life. Next door was his sister-in-law, 'Auntie' Beet, and her husband, 'Uncle' Henry Houghton. 'Uncle' Henry was worth a bob or two as he had been a rag-and-bone merchant, and had a smart little pony and trap. He took the three of us out in it once for a whole day, but never repeated the experiment. We always needed to explore the mysteries of anything new to the ultimate detail, and I think he had found our incessant questions altogether exhausting.

'Uncle' Len was a great favourite in the village. People came to him to be cheered up. The White Lion was the other end, at the top of the High Street, and he would set off, in an old flat cap which he habitually wore the wrong way round, and, of course, Tom and Dick, with a good three-quarters of an hour to spare. There he would have his pint or two – or six – of Merry and Bright (by which he meant mild and bitter) and play cribbage standing up. His maxims and his sayings were notorious and his quick wit stood out among the slower, rustic humour which characterized the local brand. We three were skilful mimics of owls and would summon tawny owls to the nursery windowsill by hooting at them. 'When I hears boys', said 'Uncle' Len, 'I thinks they's owls. But when I hears owls, I know they's boys!' He had a favourite little song which he never finished. It started: 'There's a hole in mother's stocking where the birds all love to go . . .' Another

snatch deserves repeating in full as it ranks almost with Carroll and
Lear:

> Now tomorrow is the day when they march through the City,
> With his hands tied behind him and he asks for no pity;
> Is there anybody here, from the East to St Patrick's?
> When they tied old Billy Murphy
> To the banks of Smitheramock, Smitheramock,
> Fisti-fisti-foodle-um-a-dum,
> Ri-fo, the diddle-i-do! Hi!

The last three lines we would repeat competitively as quickly as we
could, whoever reaching 'Hi!' first being declared the winner. There
was an Indian Love Song as well which I remember perfectly, but it
would look quite indecipherable written down.

'Uncle' Len's' was a safety valve where one could go for a laugh or a
chat about Life or simply to have a good swear. Our oaths shaped
themselves into an esoteric vocabulary of our own. Retribution was
swift for conventional swear-words and invariably painful. Time
honoured justifications like 'I heard Daddy say it', merely made it
worse, especially if it happened to be true. I always sympathized with
Lars Porsena when 'by the Nine Gods he swore' – he probably needed
it at the time and I'm sure he felt better afterwards. What he actually
said I could never find out. So our oaths, though holding to the general
spirit of the thing, were not bona fide swear-words and could be used
with impunity. 'You silly blummer!' had the genuine ring without the
risk. The pretty Lancashire village of Bolton-by-Bowland provided a
favourite. It is pronounced by all but the tourist and the incurably posh
as Bolton-be-Bolland. 'Well, I'll be Bolland!', said with feeling, was
as satisfactory an expletive as we ever invented.

We would help 'Uncle' Len to landscape his little garden, doing the
jobs that Tom and Dick couldn't cope with, though these were
amazingly few and mostly near the ground. Rustic fences, arches and a
pergola were made with split hazel lengths, later covered with
rambling roses. Little concrete walls edged the paths, moulded
between boards and left to set. The mixing was one of our jobs. Horse
manure, to our surprise and approval, was an ingredient. The concrete
eventually became covered in moss and lichens which tempered its
starkness. 'Auntie' Ethel, generously built with a pout like Gladys
Henson, would bring us out enamel jugs of cold tea, which is much

nicer than it sounds and just the thing in hot weather. Though no social historian, then or now, but an incorrigible theorizer, I became aware through the three Ethels who were close to me of the workings of fashion in Christian names. The great aunts, who ranged from the Saki type to the scattier Wodehouse ones, all had mid-Victorian names like the ladies in the Gilbert and Sullivans; Ethel, Alice, Ella, Edith and such. A generation later these had passed to the daughters of the cooks and parlourmaids who had been in service with them, and a few passed on to the third generation who hated the names for being ugly. Since the last war and the disappearance of the servant, the influence has moved via the cinema screen to the television. Ask the schoolteachers and they will tell you their classes are crammed today with little Waynes and Darrens, Dianes and Jeanettes (whatever happened to Diana and Janet?). I'd be surprised if there's an Ethel among them.

'Uncle' Len gave us all little brass badges to wear in the lapel. These were in the form of a tiny hand giving the cheerful Lambeth Walk thumbs-up sign. At the time I looked on the thumbs-up badges as the marks of membership of a rather comfortable little club. I saw in later years that for this dauntless man who, though often racked with pain, yet uncomplainingly radiated mirth, hope and enthusiasm, the emblem neatly summed up his philosophy of life.

'Uncle' Len reared our jackdaw, a half-naked little waif who had been blown out of a tree in 'the Walks', a bit of surviving parkland surrounding the newt pond at the back of the church. Jack came back to us when, against all odds, he had grown big enough to survive out of 'intensive care'. You can't house-train jackdaws. He would sit on a dining chair back with a newspaper on the floor below, which guaranteed cleanliness to a certain extent. He was banned from the house at night and when indulging his passion for blackcurrants as the results were indelible. I wore a special jacket for Jack. When meeting someone for the first time, unless held tightly, he would fly on to their heads and christen them. We had to be constantly on the alert. I lost my heart entirely to this extrovert comedian with his mischievous, speedwell-blue eyes. It was my job to feed him, which in the early stages involved cracking snails and mincing worms and ramming the mess down his insistent gape, for although fully fledged, he was still a baby. Growing flight feathers are protected in a waxy wrapping which is sloughed off in flaky shards, getting up your nose and making you sneeze. I also had to muck out the wooden cage every morning and scrub it with disinfectant. His cage stood open in the back porch all day but he would go and roost there at night, whereupon the door was fastened to keep intruders out rather than Jack in. He was completely fearless – young jackdaws have to be taught what enemies to avoid – but he had an aversion to cats. One malevolent black-and-white Tom with a bull head, a single eye and an ear missing, we had named Burglar. He was Jack's especial foe. On spotting a cat in the garden, Jack would give a high pitched rattle and dart after the animal, landing on its back with his claws dug in. Then would follow an exhilarating rodeo with Jack in full cry riding the witless cat as it rushed round the garden, its jockey springing nicely into the air as it dived through the hedge to safety. No, we weren't much bothered with cats. Jack would sit on my shoulder chattering importantly or cleaning the spaces between my teeth – a job which he took particular pride in. He was infallible in the outfield playing cricket. We would play 'boundaries' with fresh peas and he never missed a catch. As a batsman he showed little promise.

I must confess to shameful twinges of jealousy whenever 'Uncle' Len came to visit on his way to the Lion. Though generally loyal, as soon as Jack heard the drumming of Tom and Dick he would yelp with frenzied excitement, dancing and scuttling to his old nurse. Straight up Tom and Dick and up on to his shoulder. 'Uncle' Len was his first love and Jack was utterly devoted to him. He lived with us until well after we went away to school. Vanity, we thought, was eventually his undoing. He would spend hours strutting up and down the running board of the blue Triumph, talking and displaying to his reflection. Mirrors fascinated him. One day the gardener left the cover off the water-butt. We needed rain water for washing our hair as the tap water was so hard the soap wouldn't lather. At least the wartime soap. We used to make our own as soap was 'on points'; red, pungent, solid carbolic in big tin trays. Hence the rain water. Once you had strained out the pollywoggles (our name for the various wriggling gnat larvae) you had beautiful soft water. Because of Jack's narcissistic tendency (once we had to rescue him, furious and bedraggled, when he jumped in) a lid was made out of an old Lazy Susan, a circular, revolving tray which had retired from service at the nursery tea-table. This time nobody was about and the lid was off and Jack met a watery end.

We had many birds over the years, casualties of tree felling or natural accident. Two baby jays from Mr Fuller were wholly delightful. We christened them Ike and Mike. General Eisenhower was a hero of the time, leading the final liberation and the fight to Berlin. Little round badges proclaiming 'I like Ike' were all the rage. We added 'and Mike' to ours, avoiding suspicions of partiality. They were alike as twin peas except that Mike had a damaged foot and was not as agile as his brother. When I fed them, Ike was the more demanding and got his first. I discovered that when I turned my back to get Mike's share, Ike would deftly change places on the perch and get fed again. After this I put them on opposite ends of the perch, about a yard apart. Even then I had to be quick as he would sidle up to the other end when I took my eyes off him. Baby owls would turn up, knowing and lovable with their fluffy clumsiness and direct stare, and once a kestrel who never made friends with anybody.

We were a home to any orphan though most were already dying and left us as abruptly as they came. Starlings are full of character and make friendly pets. Indeed, they used to be known as the 'poor man's dog'. There were terrible old traditions around, though, like if you slit a starling's tongue with a sixpence it will learn to talk. The cruelty of some country lads in those days was unbelievable. It wasn't the London evacuees either, who 'couldn't be expected to know any better' and generally got blamed for everything. We would find clutches of nestlings with their heads wrenched off and scores of frogs along the River Beane, bellies ripped open. The frogs had been blown up with straws until they burst. One young criminal plucked clean a baby partridge, live, for fun. Taking down a straw stack caused the exodus of colonies of rats. They would make for the river and boys would chase after them with forked hazel thumbsticks. The rat was pinned down by the neck, picked up by the base of the tail and dropped into a deep galvanized tank. In the evening the men's terriers would be put in, singly, for a measured number of seconds, and bets would be placed on the number of rats killed by each dog. Some of the dogs would be badly hurt. There are many criticisms levelled at television for the corruption of children and the erosion of social values, some not without point, but if television has spread an awareness of the fragility and preciousness of all wildlife around us, and I think it has, then I for one am willing to tolerate much of the rest.

Badgers were long established though secretive members of our wildlife society and a badgerwatch was a favourite Birdsall entertainment. An alternative route to St John's Wood was provided by Dirty Lane. This was its accredited title, not one of our own nicknames, and pertinent too for it was a clay quagmire in wet weather. Dirty Lane flanked a line of chalk pits, honeycombed with badger burrows and the sets were full of tenants. Badger watching is not difficult if you have patience and an eye to wind direction. They are short sighted but long in the nose. They are mostly nocturnal but they will roam miles on a night's hunting, and that means an early start when it is still quite light. The old boar would come out first. After a course of tentative sniffs, he would sit down on his hunkers in the evening sun like a polar bear at the zoo. Then he would begin to scratch. For the height of ecstasy in action, give me a scratching badger. His long digging claws would rake and harrow, sending his loose skin into vibrating rolls with an enjoyment visibly infectious. We would take friends to watch the badgers and we, stifling giggles, would watch the watchers. First an exploratory fumble – an armpit, or the back of a neck – and soon the spectators would be scratching away like fun with Old Brock just winning on points. After half an hour or so of this, he would decide the coast was clear and, poking his nose into the hole, with an inaudible signal would summon up the cubs. They must have been just short of the entrance, weeing with impatience, for out they would tumble like children let out of school, biting and rolling about and playing catch-as-catch-can and all in silence. The old man, meanwhile, quickly left the scene, following a ditch which ran close to us, and was gone for the night. Other adults would appear, some keeping an eye on the cubs, others, young males we thought, making off on their own errands. Approaching darkness would end the entertainment for us and we would hurry home and leave them to it. I live near a few badgers today and get just as much fun from them and from scratching friends as ever I used to.

We would often comb the Dirty Lane chalk pits in a vain search for chalkland butterflies such as the Chalkhill Blue, but to find the nearest chalkland proper, where the chalk lies thick all over, three or four inches below the surface, and only real lime-loving plants will flourish, we had to visit Royston Heath, ten miles away. Not, you may think, a significant distance, but in those days it was remote as distant Ophir or the still vex'd Bermoothes. We were limited to the mileage our feet could take us and still get home for tea, though we were usually dusty and late when we did. Admittedly, we could roam wild within this range. There were few roads and there was virtually no traffic to speak of, apart from intermittent army convoys which could often maroon us on the wrong side of the High Street for hours when lorries and tanks and gun carriers rumbled nose-to-tail past the village green on their way south to the build-up for for the famous Second Front. Normally it was very quiet. In winter we would all toboggan unhindered down the High Street on the impacted snow. England was a wider place in those days. Ethel's father, a soft spoken, thoughtful old man, had never been to London (though Ethel had actually cycled the thirty-five miles). To hear him, he could have been talking of Rome or Washington. People didn't go far from home. A roll of honour was still in existence in the church archives from, I think, Agincourt. Most of the names were recorded again on the memorial for the Great War and in some cases, local legend had it, the families were still in the same cottages. I longed for the day when my horizon could be extended by a bike.

One hot July afternoon in 1943 we persuaded Dad to take us to Royston Heath in quest of the Chalkhill Blue. This was the first time I really grasped the concept of 'habitat' and the interdependence of the earth and the plants and the butterflies which live on them. The caterpillars of the Chalkhill Blue feed on the horseshoe vetch and bird'sfoot trefoil, both common plants on chalk and limestone, but found nowhere else. Chalkland is ideal butterflying country, for the plants are mostly very low growing and even the grass is short. The scents are appetizing, like a good herby chicken stuffing, mostly wild thyme and marjoram, their mauve-pink scattered with pale blue of the little scabious and yellow of the rock roses and here and there a darker purple of the wild orchid. We found the bee orchid on Royston Heath, slender spikes hung with remarkably life-like bumble bees. I caught my first Chalkhill Blue as soon as I got out of the car. They were there in abundance. A new species, and all over the place. 'There are myriads of them!', I cried, a phrase which tickled Dad for he reminded me of it even last year. To explain, I had often been told not to exaggerate when talking of 'millions' and this poetic quantity seemed to fit the bill.

The Chalkhill Blue is a blue of its own, pale and silvery as though dusted with the chalk it lives on, and rather bigger than the Common Blue. His lady is dark brown with the edge of a white petticoat peeping out at the borders. Their undersides are pale and chalky with the ringed spots affected by all the Blues. They are quite strong fliers, keeping close to the ground as do most of the chalkland butterflies. There is little shelter on such heathland from winds or predators and it is useful to be able to drop suddenly into the grass roots when things get dangerous. We caught all the Chalkhill Blues we needed on the first occasion we met them, releasing all but perfect, undamaged specimens. Our standard number for a species was six: two male, two female and one of each set upside-down to show the underside. Conventionally one did not set moths as 'undersides' though I don't know why as some were very pretty.

On the way back from Royston Heath, turning left at Slip End into lanes like tunnels where pollard oaks, victims of long dead farmers' rights of 'lop and top', closed up the canopy overhead from the height of the steep banks, was a tiny, unfrequented pub called the Swan, kept by a knotty little man, as old as the oaks, who in his loneliness also kept a canary. He was forever digging up bits of Roman armour when he lifted his potatoes. The canary trilled happily, a bright contrast to the blackened rafters from which its cage hung in the dark little bar parlour. The story was told how a passing salesman had called in one day, an expert on cage birds, and said the canary could not be expected to survive many months in such a smoky atmosphere and what a downright shame. The landlord thanked him politely and replied that very like he was right and the bird had only been there thirteen years and if he noticed him ailing, he'd take him out for a bit of fresh air.

The lively sport at Royston must have appealed to Dad, for shortly afterwards we made our first of many excursions to Pegsdon Downs. This was an enchanted tract of chalky countryside, steeped in pre-history, with magic names like Sharpenhoe Clappers, Pulsatilla Banks, Beacon Hill and Barn Hole, Knocking Hoe and Lilley Hoo and the Tingley Wood. Tim was inspired to add another poem to his growing auto-anthology:

> Pegsdon Downs are far from Towns;
> They're more like Pegsdon Up and Downs . . .

The terrain we explored was about ten square miles of chalk downs and dry valleys. Dozing in an express coach travelling down the M1 recently and approaching Luton, I woke to a vivid sense of *déjà vu*. It came to me with a shock that I recognized the landmarks either side of me, and indeed the motorway has sliced its way through our old butterflying haunts of half a lifetime ago. Vandalism! At least, this was my first reaction. But, on reflection, once the dust has settled from the initial violation and nature calmed down again, the motorways afford a fair chance of the habitats surrounding them remaining unvisited and undisturbed, simply because you're not allowed to stop.

One of the features to jog my memory was the Sharpenhoe Clappers which once sounded to us like an obscure complaint associated with elderly gardeners. It was a ridge made conspicuous by its bold angularity among the roundness, crested by a knife edge of tall trees which looked as if they would bang together in windy weather. Barn Hole was the steepest of the dry valleys with a floor like a wide, flat running track guarded in Cretan style by a monstrous bull. Knocking Hoe was a rounded knoll on the end of Pulsatilla Banks where you could plainly see the terraces which stone-age man cut out to grow his crops and a distinct square field which he must have ploughed, where the grass grew slightly darker. He had also left a well-marked trackway marching up Lilley Hoo where he would have once driven his cattle. On Lilley Hoo we caught the Little Blue (I know that as it became part of Tim's lost poem). This is notable among the British butterflies as Rutland was among the counties, for being the smallest. I think the Little Blue still survives where Rutland, alas, does not except in the memories of countless schoolboys like myself who treasured it as the sole fact of English geography one could be certain of, like 1066 being the only memorable date.

The Small Blue, to give it its more usual name, has a wingspan of just over three-quarters of an inch. Both male and female are a sooty brown colour, but the male has a blue flash fanning out from the body which varies in size in individuals. His lady is petite but drab. Underneath they are pale grey-blue with rows of black dots. Unpleasant it may be to slander any butterfly, especially such a diminutive one, and it is unquestionably a habit they grow out of as they get older, but we did read somewhere that the caterpillars of the Small Blue have a tendency to cannibalism. Probably that carp Kirby. He's always seeing the worst in people. They certainly were never common and if they spent their time eating one another that wasn't surprising. The butterflies also seemed to like railway banks – I later found them along the London and North Eastern Railway near

Stevenage and one part of the London, Midland and Scottish in North Yorkshire.

Climbing up the steep glacial slopes out of Barn Hole, where you couldn't sit down for a rest because of a penetrating carpet of minute, flat thistles, and the Minotaur waited for you to roll down to the bottom again, we found another new species. This was the Silver Spotted Skipper. He is fractionally larger than the common Large Skipper, and rather more handsome, the fulvous brown and black on the upperside having a glossier contrast. Underneath, the hindwings are a sap green blotched with the spots which give the name. Not true silver, as in the larger Fritillaries, but a pearly white which gives a good imitation. Indeed, our old friend W. Egmont Kirby M.D. calls it the Pearl Skipper, and for once we felt he had a point. Perhaps we had been a little harsh in our judgement. After all, a man who can also write *Hoffmann's Young Beetle-Collector's Handbook* (and he did) can't be wrong all the time. The Silver Spotted Skipper was the aristocrat of the Skippers, a skilled flier who was very difficult to catch, especially on the prickly slopes of Barn Hole.

Another beauty with real silver spots flew here, the Dark Green Fritillary, which we have already met when Tim thought he'd got a Peacock. The only distinction between this and the other large Fritillaries is on the underside, where the hindwing is dusted with dark green under the oval spots with their metallic lustre. The High Brown never left the woods, so if you caught one here it was bound to be a Dark Green. They would fly in a straight line with tremendous power and speed, keeping a couple of feet above the short turf. You would have to spot one coming towards you while still some distance away, take a swift bearing, position yourself and wait for it to reach you. One stroke was all you were allowed, for if you missed with the net it would outdistance you with disdainful ease when you turned and gave chase. Every capture of a Dark Green Fritillary was a rare triumph.

Lower down there was a small colony of Marsh Fritillaries, the first of the smaller Fritillaries we were to come across. The habitat could not be described as marshy, but the meadows must have been fairly damp. The small Fritillaries are little more than half the size of the three large ones and don't have the silver spots underneath. They are very decorative all the same and it is a temptation to take too many for they are easy to catch and present in fair numbers, living as they do in friendly little communities. The Marsh Fritillary is not as bright a chestnut orange as the others and most of the dice-box spots have merged into bands. It is also decorated with bands of pale, straw coloured patches, like small leaded lights in a stained-glass window. The underside is similar and surprisingly shiny. W. E. Kirby, quick to fasten on anyone's bad points, called it the Greasy Fritillary, but this was Kirby back in his old style and hardly fair.

Tingley Wood, near Highdown, was another splendid oak wood where the Purple Emperor was reputed once to have flown, but we never saw it there. A grand butterfly wood, though it never yielded anything that we hadn't already met nearer home. One incident, however, stands out in my memory, as illustrating those legends that one constantly reads about but never witnesses. Driving slowly along the lane bordering Tingley Wood, we came upon a large flock of sparrows covering the way. This was common enough where grain had been spilt from a cart and the birds usually flew clear just in time. Not one moved so Dad stopped the car. In the middle of the flock was a weasel, somersaulting and cartwheeling in an astounding gymnastic display and his audience was, quite literally, spellbound. We hooted. The weasel stopped in mid-pirouette and saw us in the same moment, grabbed the nearest sparrow and was off. The other sparrows came to their senses slowly as though waking from a trance – which I suppose they were – and eventually our path was clear to move on.

It was around this time that a sort of cousin, John, and his sister, Barbara (they were in fact half-brother and sister to 'Aunt' West who owned the Bible with the black Jesus), first came to stay. They lived in the middle of the Ashdown Forest. John had our enthusiasm for any kind of natural history but he had never concentrated on butterflies and moths. Needless to say, the craze got him. I shall introduce John properly later on, but for the moment his brief appearance is necessary as it was through him that I began to grasp that not all the butterflies that I had never seen were on this account rarities, nor all that I was familiar with commonly found everywhere else. It stemmed from our favourite game on wet days when we tended to stay indoors. There was a ridiculous little tune then popular called 'Butterflies in the Rain'. Or rather, the tune is pretty and harmless enough – it is the title that is ridiculous. You don't see butterflies in the rain. They hide away dismally and keep their wings dry. There are a few moths, like the

Silver Y and the Humming-Bird Hawk which visit the flowers quite unconcernedly in a veritable downpour (they hover with wings beating at speeds which render them a blur, so no doubt they keep dry that way), but not butterflies. So in wet weather in default of the real thing we would pore over the pictures. Tim and I were showing John the *Observer's Book*, rather boastfully I fear, stabbing a finger ('We've got that one! And we've got that one!') at each page showing a species already in our collection. John couldn't cap this, but he chose an 'I've seen that one!' or 'We get that one round us!' technique. Quite a few of these, like the Grayling and the Speckled Wood came into the list of butterflies I had never seen and I had suspicions of a leg pull. I found out later how acute his observation must have been, for, without any special interest to concentrate his attention, he had been right on all counts.

It was some seven years before we came across the other downland butterflies, when we had moved to the south coast at Eastbourne. The grassy slopes at the foot of Beachy Head, the cliff tops to Birling Gap and the sweep of chalk between Jevington and Alfriston were new hunting grounds to be explored. The plough hadn't raped the ancient hills then, peregrines and stone curlew were a familiar sight and a coastguard still patrolled the cliffs on a white charger. Three new species, all of them very individual characters, were added to our list.

The Marbled White is not a White but belongs to the Brown family. In the days when such was the custom, it was known lugubriously, but very appropriately, as the Half Mourner, for it is dressed in sombre black and white. The first time we met the Marbled Whites, they were swarming in the rough long grasses. In some years, for a brief period of their season, some butterflies appear in huge numbers, whereas in most years they are thinner on the ground. This is true of course of the migrants, who often arrive in hordes from the Continent, but it also happens to residents like the Marbled White. A speculation we always found intriguing was whether we would recognize a new species in flight – would it look immediately like its pictures? Not that we doubted the illustrations. Here were no Holbeins gilding a Flemish Mare, but faithful reporters of truth to the best of their talents. The confusion was that a living, flying butterfly presents superimposed images of both the upperside and the underside. We would often make a toy from a sheet of card, drawing on one side a canary, say, and on the reverse a barred cage. A loop of string was threaded through the

93

edges and by twisting and pulling the card would be made to spin rapidly whereupon the canary would appear inside the cage. This was the effect produced by a fast flying butterfly or moth. Some, like the Hawk Moths, flapped so fast that the wings were scarcely visible at all. A Peacock, with its black underside, looks heavily dark in flight, the vivid eye markings not apparent, whereas the yellow Brimstone is unmistakable. The Marbled White was straightway identifiable. Though the pale underside caused it to flicker a bit, it looked for all the world like a flying chessboard. An alarming phenomenon occurred when the white spots turned bright yellow in the cyanide jar. This faded back to the normal colour, however, when they were removed. We caught our complete series of these on first acquaintance. I have never seen the Marbled White since in such crowds.

The Grayling is the McCavity of the Brown family, an eerily flitting fawn-grey ghost. It is also the largest Satyr, spanning some two and a half inches, and flies with speed unlike the flopping flight of most of the family. Its dress conforms to the general dowdiness of the clan however, an overall dusty brown with paler ochre patches on the margins of the wings giving prominence to six of the Disney eye spots. The underside is similiar, but the hindwings are a mosaic of brown, black and white like lichen on bark. We heard somewhere that the Grayling never visited flowers, which seemed unlikely, but certainly we most often saw it, on really hot days when most people would be lying far below us on the beach like slabs of meat, alighting on patches of bare, chalky earth. The Grayling has perfected the vanishing trick. We would spot one furtively darting over the turf and abruptly settling. If we came up fairly quickly, the closed wings would present the alert 'eye' of the forewing. After a second or two the forewing would be drawn down, hiding the eye, and the butterfly would lie down almost on its side so that even its shadow disappeared. Like a plover's nest, take your eyes off and it took a search to find it again, so perfect is the camouflage. If we were late in coming up and the eye had already been hidden, the butterfly was almost impossible to find on its background of baked earth. Many times I have marked the place where a Grayling had settled, stared fixedly and failed to find it. The only resort was optimistically to plonk the net down on the place where you knew it was, usually to see the butterfly start up into visibility some six inches further on and dash away to another spot. It is strong in flight but normally only for short bursts, so one

94

could often see it alight again and the game could go on for hours.

The last of our downland company was a little gem and for my money the prettiest of our British butterflies, though beauty competitions are rather arbitrary affairs when all's said and done and they never choose my favourite as Miss World or Miss United Kingdom or whatever. The contestant here was the Adonis Blue. And well named, for Adonis was the youth beloved of the Olympian goddesses, no mean judges when it came to masculine beauty. The Victorians, never happy to leave Nature as they found it, used to make pictures of crinolined ladies or unlikely flowers using butterfly wings. My grandparents had one or two. The butterflies chosen were a large foreign species of a lustrous blue. Such was the colour of the male Adonis Blue, brilliant azure, burnished like a kingfisher and reflecting the sunlight, with a black and white fringe bordering the wings. The underside is indistinguishable at a glance from the Common Blue, and at rest with the wings closed the butterflies look identical. Once the wings open wide to the sun, and even in flight, the full glory of the male is striking and the Common Blue seems dim in comparison when they are flying together as they often do. Twice a year, in late May and again in August, the Adonis Blue could be found, though never in large numbers, fluttering among the scabious and thistle flowers, a delight to wayfarers awake enough to notice him. W. Carter Platts, an old angling crony of Gramp's, writing in one of his many fishing books about the times when nothing would take the fly, said, 'The day is never wasted on which you have seen a Kingfisher'. I felt the same, returning floury white and weary from the Downs, about the Adonis Blue.

CHAPTER SIX

Dragons, Poetry and Pigeon Shooting

Large and Small Pearl Bordered Fritillaries

IN the February of 1943 Tim caught diphtheria. He complained undramatically that it hurt where his dinner went down. At the back of his throat was a livid white curtain. In true Yorkshire style of the 'Cobbler's barns goin' bar-shod', we had never been immunized. How Patrick and I escaped infection was little short of miraculous, but might have had much to do with what, in the terse phraseology of our times, is now called 'colour coding'. All our domestic apparatus followed this system; mine was green, Tim's blue and Patrick's yellow – toothbrushes, toothmugs, flannels, combs and brushes, pens and pencils, even pos in the early stages – and we obstinately refused to use anything that was not our favourite colour. There was to my imagination, however, always something vulnerable about Tim, and I say this without hindsight. This in spite of the fact that he was undoubtedly the toughest of us, a natural athlete with an irascible temper which Patrick and I were constantly wary of. On the other hand, a phrase or incident which tickled him would send him into paroxysms of infectious laughter which well-nigh choked him and left him bright red, tear-stained and exhausted. In my recurrent nightmares about German soldiers taking over the Cottage, it was always Tim who would be shot, as a reprisal for some injudicious remark or action of defiance. I was aware that he was a conspicuously beautiful child, with his black hair, startling blue eyes and long, curling lashes, heritage of our Irish Edwards grandmother, the envy of any aspiring starlet. If this were commented on, as tactless females were wont to do, he would scowl and grimace and pull terrifying faces until they were gone.

Luckily the night that Tim felt ill was a Wednesday, when Dad came home for the night on his mid-week respite from a sleepless London. By another fortuitous coincidence, a recent patient had been the young son of Dr Levene, principal of the London Fever Hospital. It was here that Tim was straightway taken in the car, carried, to his seven-year-old disgust, like a new born infant, forbidden to move even an arm – for the strain of this cruel disease on the heart was notorious, even were the sufferer to recover. Happily, due to the chain of discovery started by Fleming at St Mary's, there are no longer any Fever Hospitals. In country districts folk still point out the lonely building that was once the 'Isolation Hospital', but as a curiosity, giving no indication of the unease the sight of it used once to evoke. The institutions sound Dickensian today, but it is not so long ago that they became obsolete. Mum had caught pneumonia as a young student nurse and was actually bled with leeches. Certainly when I was myself a Barts' student they had them still on the strength and I wouldn't be surprised to hear they were there yet.

Straight from the shoulder Dad told us, kindly but unemotionally, that Tim was very, very poorly and likely to die. He had to tell me the same thing some twenty years later with more shattering effect, when Tim was in the final stages of leukaemia. Patrick and I were inoculated with a painful regularity and throat swabs became the order of the day. The local practitioners and district nurses were brought into the fray and swabs were taken from all possible contacts in the village for somewhere, innocent and unaware, walked the carrier, unaffected by the fatal bacilli but capable of passing them on to further victims. The infamous typhus carriers of history, invariably working with food or confectionery and responsible for huge epidemics and the deaths of thousands, always seemed to me to come out of a Sherlock Holmes story, with names like 'Typhoid Mary', and 'The Wife of the Strasbourg Baker'. And indeed the hunt for the source of Tim's infection had much of the drama of a good detective story. Forests of cottonwool-tipped sticks, each in a labelled test tube, went daily to London. When no results were forthcoming, the whole process was laboriously repeated. Still no positive report from the pathologist. Dad wanted to know if the teeth had been included in the swabs. They had not. At last the lurking bacteria were found, for these were the days before 'free' dental treatment, and sets of false teeth would be worn concealing the blackened, ground down stumps of the originals, extraction being beyond the purses of most folk even if they did not lack the courage for such drastic treatment. The unknowing culprit was tracked down and even the chance contact when Tim caught the infection.

Tim spent his birthday in the Fever Hospital that year, flat on his back and devotedly nursed, forbidden even to turn over without assistance. Toys consisted of tiny pipe cleaner animals which he was allowed to lift and a clown who somersaulted along a pair of parallel bars and somehow never fell off. Patrick and I spent much time with Dr Levene. He had a capacious Noah's Ark with every animal I could imagine carved solidly in pairs out of wood. I looked at Tim's bacteria down the microscope, rather fearfully, and drew pictures of them, tiny coloured torpedo shapes like the capsules which today replace the old fashioned tablets. We were never allowed to go and talk to Tim, but on fine days his bed would be wheeled out on the balcony and we could wave at him from the tennis court below. Mum and Dad would be at his bedside in masks and white coats and point us out to him and he would manage a small wave in reply. Tim recovered, without a blemish, without a trace of cardiac damage, due to the love and skill of the nurses. His toys and treasures and many most exquisite books were all burnt, such was the virulence of diphtheria in those days. In the early summer he went to Nutley in the Ashdown Forest to convalesce.

I have already spoken of 'Aunt' West, fairy godmother, who started her nursing career alongside Mum and after completing her 'Midder' went off to the Congo as a missionary. Her long association with her Birdsall godsons started on the day of her triumphal return in 1938, as she was met at Victoria by Mum and Dad in our little Morris Eight and was to come and stay for a bit. Tim and I (Patrick had not then appeared on the scene) had been left playing quietly in the drawing room, considered safe enough at the time as the station was close by. I am told that when our devout godmother was ushered in to be introduced for the first time, we had extracted all the empty beer bottles from the sideboard and were playing ninepins with them on the carpet. Such early signs of profligacy must have sparked one of her life's missions, for she was a watchful and treasured godmother to all the Birdsalls and eventually to their children. In fact the title was a purely honorary one for some time for we were not officially christened until much later. We had our silver christening tankards, which preceded the event (mine by more than nine years) and were presents from 'Uncle' Brian who was to give me the 'peace treaty' pen. These tankards (I've still got mine) held one third of a pint. Every Sunday at the Cottage in the early 'forties, a large, wicker-covered demi-john would be filled with Simpson's dark mild ale at the White Lion and brought back for lunch. We could have as much beer as we liked in our tankards. Actually we didn't like much at the time though Tim used to pretend he did out of loyalty to Dad. At least we never drank out of daredevilry or to show off because it was always there if we wanted it. And so we didn't want it. I think that was the idea behind it – that and a source of vitamin C which was a bit scarce during the war.

The demand to be christened came, in the summer of 1944, from me: I was greatly taken with the Rector, eminent butterfly man that he was, and because I loved making music I also wanted to sing in the choir, a task regarded as an irksome chore by many of my friends who had been chosen rather than called, reversing the biblical precedent. Nine was the eligible age and I had already achieved that. Dr Greenham told me, a little diffidently, I couldn't join as I hadn't been christened. Dad was digging early potatoes when I approached him. 'Is it all right if I get christened?' He put down the fork and looked at me. 'I don't see why not.' So the new convert dashed in to tell Mum that he had to be christened and Dad said so and amazingly it was all arranged for next Sunday. I hadn't realized that Mum and West had been racking their brains for years as to how to bring the ceremony about, as the Birdsalls were as atheistic a bunch as you could find without being actively pagan. If Dad had realized he was to be host to a crowd of friends and marched to church in a collar and tie on a sweltering summer Sabbath he might not have agreed so casually. He was given no time to change his mind. We were all three done in a job lot. Being nearly ten years old and thus experienced in the Devil and all his Works, I importantly answered all my own responses, and the next Wednesday gravely attended choir practice.

During the Blitz 'Aunt' West was a district midwife in Catford and Lewisham (which also made her godmother to battalions of Cockney children between Brixton and Blackheath) and would often come to Harley Street on those occasions when Dad needed a Sister present to chaperone a consultation or a bit of minor treatment. She also arrived to look after us whenever Mum had to stay in London for periodic bouts of treatment. Ethel really looked after us but she wasn't that much older than we were, and 'Aunt' West would rule the roost. Mum went through every form of therapy currently fashionable for arthritis; gold injections, bee-stings, electrical treatment and they were forever coming up with new ones. Nothing did much good for very long.

'Aunt' West would have running battles with Dad at the week-ends, usually with her head stuck out of the bathroom window overlooking the back garden. 'Sam! Why do you always light your bonfire when I've hung my washing out?' 'Why do you always hang your ruddy washing out when I've lit my bonfire?' He had a point, we felt. There never was a moment while 'Aunt' West was around when the garden wasn't garlanded with washing, and she'd often come out among the vegetables and wrest the shirt off Dad's back to put it in the tub. 'Cleanliness is next to Godliness', she would say smugly, and surely she should have known.

West's father, 'Uncle' Jack, was a tall, lean Patrician with a beard and an eye like an Old Testament prophet, though the fierce aspect was on the surface only. He had married again after West's mother had died, and John and Barbara were the children of his second marriage and so became West's half-brother and sister. 'Uncle' Jack ran the telephone exchange at Nutley where Tim had gone to recuperate, a thickly carpeted room where we were never allowed, and where we would sometimes glimpse him through the open door, with earphones and a kind of black Viking's drinking horn strapped under his chin. The house was, by virtue of its official business, as hushed as Harley Street with something of the same secretive atmosphere, and as most of our amusements were relatively high spirited, we spent most of the time in the forest or in the garage. Patrick and Ethel and I joined Tim later in the summer while Mum spent a protracted time battling with her latest course of therapy. We travelled there on a green Southdown coach along with a white kitten we had perversely christened Sambo. The house is still there, though the road is now a busy route to the coast, next to a large green, with its white fence like a child's playpen on the apex of the roof, a parapet with a wonderful view of miles of the Ashdown forest beyond. We were allowed up to it for rare visits. 'Uncle' Jack was also something of a local printer ('do-it-yourself' was invented during the war as there was nobody around to do it for you) and notices of fêtes and funerals were duplicated for the village church using a tray of jelly made unappetizingly from seaweed and purple ink which shone iridescently green in the light and got everywhere.

John was a couple of years or so older than I, long and gangling and similarly stage-struck. Everyone was giving concerts for the war effort, from village halls where you paid about sixpence, to the National Gallery where it was free and we once listened to Dame Myra Hess. So we gave concerts in the garage. They were free as at current prices we would only have collected about half-a-crown anyway. Most of our material was borrowed from Sandy Powell backed by 'Open up dem Pearly Gates' on an old wind-up gramophone.

'I want to join the Regiment.'

'The King's?'
'No, the Queen's.'
'Why?'
'Because I am an Old Woman!'

Not uproarious stuff but we got our laughs. I was the feed. Parts were written in to suit the performers. We were all involved though Barbara was reluctant and preferred a good book. Patrick, at five, had difficulty with lines but was good for 'skins' parts and made a convincing cat. Tim and John were the natural comedians while the rest of us kept the gramophone wound up and manned the tabs – a makeshift curtain on a string which could be relied on to collapse at moments of tension. I wrote an epic drama about an eccentric professor and a phenomenal secret weapon, inspired by the weapon itself which was a broken gadget with a bellows once used for puffing burning sulphur fumes into wasps' nests. The plot was a serious one but, although I have forgotten development and denoument, I recall to my chagrin that in performance it earned more laughs than any of the comic sketches.

Off stage, hospitals and medicine provided boundless topics for digression, much as they did with our elders, the womenfolk anyway, especially as Tim had just emerged from his ordeal. We would endeavour to outsoar each other in boastful flights of blood-curdling fancy. The pinnacle of repulsiveness was achieved by John who described in lurid olfactory detail a mud-like medicine called Hogsbelly which he had been compelled to take for weeks on end by the tablespoonful. One didn't know which was the more admirable, his courage or his inventiveness. I don't think there are any nasty medicines now, the pills have all been gilded.

Nearby East Grinstead boasted a cinema where we would go on occasion, collecting further material for concerts or mimicry – Will Hay or George Formby or the Hulberts in complicated uniformed fantasies. The long, terraced steps of the High Street were crowded with airmen and their girls sitting in the sunshine. Sometimes in the cinema we would see a little group of grotesquely mutilated faces, the patients of Gillies and McIndoe, old friends and colleagues of both Mum and Dad, who were painstakingly restoring some semblance of human conformity to the tortured faces and limbs of survivors of 'The Few'. *The Electric Man* was a horror film which seemed rather tame in contrast and we were insensitive enough to find it uproariously funny.

Some time later the cinema received a direct hit and most of the audience was killed at once.

Mostly we would cross the road with a picnic and disappear miles into the forest for the day. The forest was not what I had expected, basing my experience on Grimms' Fairy Tales and the dark phantasms of Snow White and the Wizard of Oz. Trees there were in plenty but also wide acres of heather, gorse and bracken and low-growing scrub with the ubiquitous willowherb forming small forests of its own. Huge wood ants built big, shaggy hills of shifting twig and straw, rather like the All Bran we were given for breakfast to 'keep us regular'. Adders were not uncommon, sunning themselves on banks and knolls, but they slid out of the way noiselessly as one approached. Tales were told of man-eating soldier ants as big as your thumb and monstrous serpents which might surely live somewhere in this wild expanse, but it merely added relish to the expeditions. Patrick found a bright lizard which escaped his grasp. 'It's lizarded off!', said he, adding yet another new-minted word to our collection. One night we heard the intermittent roar of a wounded Wellington bomber coming in low over the forest in the distance. It was on fire and we could see it plainly from the windows. We took a rough bearing and determined to set out in search of it in the morning as soon as we could get away. After a long trek we found it, more by luck than accurate judgement, though it had left a long trail of broken timber before it had hit the glade. Other, official, parties had been and gone before us, for there was no sign of crew, alive or dead. We never discovered whether there were survivors. I should be able to describe to you the blood and blistered camouflage and twisted metal – I remember it had broken its back and lay flopped like a shot pheasant – but it is trivial, human details that stay clearly in my mind's eye: torn fragments of a balaclava helmet, a single charred leather glove, a spilt packet of sandwiches which the ants had got to and the whole with an air of being deserted ages ago like a long empty house.

The Ashdown Forest yielded three more butterflies, though it was in no way their exclusive domain. The earliest, which after the first breathless encounter (the excitement of a new species always produced this respiratory seizure in me) proved to be common, was a dappled and dainty member of the Brown Satyrs, the Speckled Wood. Flying in and out of the outskirts of woods or entrances to rides, the Speckled Wood mimics the spots and shadows cast by the filtering sunshine, brown with pale buff spots and blotches, two alert eye spots on the forewings and a string of them on the hindwings. Unlike most butterflies, it didn't seem to favour bright sunlight, but spent most of the time in the half light among the trees. Whenever you needed a rest from the sun and turned into the kinder shadows, each opening in the trees or gap where a fence could be climbed had its guardian Speckled Wood which had claimed the small patch as its own exclusive territory. We never saw the Speckled Wood in Hertfordshire. Why this should be was not clear, for the food-plant was common grasses, in plentiful supply, and the woods seemed ideal. Strangely, I visited my old haunts some six or seven years back to put some flowers on Tim's grave as I was in the neighbourhood and I called briefly on St John's. The first thing that greeted me was a Speckled Wood butterfly.

The other two forest dwellers were the little Pearl Bordered Fritillaries, Large and Small. They are so alike that they need close examination to tell them apart, but that is when you are looking at preserved specimens. In life it is a little easier, for the Large Pearl Bordered Fritillary flies in late May and the Small Pearl Bordered in early July. Only for a short time in June did we find them both together. The size isn't much help because there's only about a tenth of an inch difference in the wingspan, and the 'Large' and 'Small' don't refer to the pearl border, for both have a border of seven pearls on the underside of each hindwing. There is also a long, egg-shaped pearl in the middle. The Small has three or four pearly patches surrounding this, but the Large has only the single pearl, like the one of Great Price. Count the pearls and you had your answer. These glowing little foxy brown butterflies were quite common fluttering over the sunny woodland glades, and the Small Pearl Bordered Fritillary also frequented more open country especially if there were reeds and a certain amount of damp. They were a memorable feature of long, hot days spent in the wild among the bracken and bell heather, far from hooting motors and toiling men. Counting pearls on little Fritillaries has not been one of the most productive occupations of my life, but I certainly number it as one of the most delightful. We went too far with our fantasies, for we invented a dragon which roamed the forest and lived at the bottom of Honey-Pot Lane. This preyed on Patrick's imagination and he began to have dread nightmares, culminating in a long, frightening attack of asthma, a condition he had been prone to since babyhood. We were told off severely for our silly stories and, much chastened, buried the dragon and the boa constrictors and the anthropophagous ants for ever.

Tim returned with us to the Cottage in time for the harvest and the busiest days in the village calendar. Harvest time opened up our terrain with a broad sweep. Acre after acre, inaccessible to us all spring and summer, became wide, unaccustomed tracts of short stubble, stippled with leaning stooks, three in a bundle, waiting to be gathered when thoroughly dry. The fields were cut with the reaper-and-binder in those days, its arms clacking and flailing like some quixotic windmill, gathering the standing corn in bundles and disgorging the sheaves spasmodically from its side, trussed securely with the binder-twine which it spun somewhere in its versatile interior. The men would follow behind and stand them up to dry. A field was cut spirally inwards, starting at the perimeter, so at the end of the day there would remain a small island in the middle. Into this had crept all the animals and flight-reluctant birds, clinging to the delusive protection of the stalks. When the dwindling haven reached the size of a blanket, its prisoners would all break cover at once; rabbits, hares, partridges, maybe a fox or a badger, dashing in panic across the unfamiliar open for the hedges surrounding it.

More excitement was to follow. The heralds of the high-jinks to come were the threshing machines, monstrous steam engines, black and brazen, which would lumber noisily up the High Street bound for one farm or another, even more exciting than steam rollers, attended by a retinue of alien, raven haired acolytes – Romanies whom some still mysteriously called 'the Egyptians'. The long, flat wagons, empty, ready-made stages for whatever impromptu melodrama took our fancy of the moment, moved out with their teams from the farms to the cut fields. Were you forced to walk the plank or bail out from your burning Wellington, the pace was slow enough and the platform low enough for you to scramble valiantly back and try the game again. Harvesting days would turn us dark brown, naked as savages. Undulating muscles of the men forking the stooks up high flickered with purple shadows and we all had a blue bloom like the sloes. The journey home saw us nesting in the top of the swaying load, or, if discovered and turfed off, squeezed into the framework at the rear of the wagon, bumping happily a few inches above the dust and stones of the road retreating underneath us.

'We never come home without something' was our perennial motto. One day Patrick found a baby rabbit. It was not a fluffy, cotton-tailed, Beatrix Potter rabbit, but a blind, black, naked, groping little casualty of the reaper-and-binder – rabbits, like cats and dogs, are born in lairs and so protected, unlike hares and deer and cows and horses who are born precariously above ground and must be wide-eyed and ready for the off, minutes after arriving. Rabbits were often lulled into a false security by the cornfields and nested in shallow digs rather than the well-established warrens.

'I've always wanted a rabbit!'

'This one's too young. It's not left its mother.'

Patrick was indignant. 'Its mother's left *it!* I've always wanted one.'

'It's wounded. P'raps its mother'll come back', I added feebly.

'Always and always! One of my own!'

Tim and I could see that this little scrap was not going to live much longer and at length we persuaded Patrick to leave it, now wrapped in his handkerchief, in peace. Half way across the next field we turned. Patrick was tramping bravely along a few paces behind. Two tears the size of sparrow's eggs lodged on his cheeks but still he came on manfully. Suddenly I couldn't take it. 'All right, let's bring it home! It can have the jackdaw cage.' Patrick sped unerringly back to the spot where he had left his rabbit.

'It'll have to have a name.' Tim was a stickler for tradition. All our vagrant animals were solemnly christened, together with neighbouring piglets and other people's cats.

'It's weed all over my handkerchief!'

'That's his name! Wee Hank!' said Tim. Our spirits soared.

Wee Hank was dead when we got him home and, as we had feared, we had merely postponed the pain for Patrick by being soft. However, nothing cheers one up like a good funeral and the mortal remains of one tiny bunny, still shrouded in Patrick's handkerchief, were placed in a shoe box and with due ceremony interred in the special graveyard reserved for such unfortunates beneath the snowberry bushes behind the back fence.

After September, when the buddleia is full of the *Vanessa* tribe feeding on the last sweets of the summer, the butterfly season begins to quieten down. Not so noticeably the moths, for they mostly avoid the sunlight and are happy if night temperatures are still warm. There is an October moth and a November moth and even a December moth which I have often seen fluttering in the car headlights in mid-Yorkshire winter. But by and large the close season is approaching when caterpillars will have eaten their fill and spun their final cocoons or burrowed into peat to pupate at the bottoms of the cages and all sun-loving creatures have sensibly bedded down, each to his own fashion, for the long winter's sleep. Then is the time for butterfly men to take stock, to pack away the nets in mothballs, leaving one to hand just in case and to remind one of times to come round again, and to breathe deeply in preparation for evenings with feet stretched before the inglenook fire, remembering with advantages what feats they did in the summer so recently past. One was not entirely inactive, for there were chrysalids like the Lime Hawk to dig for in the soft mould at the base of the trees before the frosts came, in intervals between gathering late mushrooms or collecting conkers.

Patrick was the Conkering King (the hymn always made us giggle). In shattered Germany in 1947, where our parents lived for six months in Hamburg, the conkers were truly magnificent. Dad had been called up, ironically, just after the war ended and was stationed there in the Royal Army Medical Corps as senior Ear, Nose and Throat Surgeon at the 94th B.A.O.R. (British Army of the Rhine) Hospital. We spent our holidays there. Returning to prep school in mid-autumn, Patrick brought home a huge box of these champions which proved so deadly that no one would play him. Unbeknown to us, Major Birdsall had secreted our three pairs of Zeiss binoculars (purchased for cigarettes – the only effective currency) at the bottom of the box. Patrick insisted on declaring his German Conkers. The Customs Officer considered the case and then pronounced that it would be all right provided he wasn't intending to sell them. Patrick trotted on happily and Dad must have breathed a sigh of relief. Judge of his consternation when his young smuggler turned and went back to the desk! Fagin must have suffered the same pangs when Oliver defected. At last Patrick regained the attention of the Customs and Excise. 'Is it all right to swop them?', he enquired anxiously. He was smilingly reassured.

One essential piece of equipment was Messrs Watkins and Doncaster's relaxing tin. When moths and butterflies die, the wing muscles and the bodies stiffen, after a day or so, into a permanent rigor. This is what happens on the setting board so that after a fortnight or so the braces are removed and the specimen is transferred to the cabinet, its wings displayed for ever in the right position. If an insect is left, however, setting becomes impossible as the wings become brittle and will not open. The relaxing tin contained a felt pad which was dampened with Watkins and Doncaster's Patent Relaxing Fluid. (Dad claimed to have his own relaxing fluid, distilled by John Jameson, but it was too precious to use on the butterflies.) Hermetically sealed in the tin on layers of cottonwool, butterflies and moths remained in a pliable state indefinitely. In the height of the season it was often impossible to keep pace with setting all the accumulating specimens, and by transferring them to the magic tin, this part of the collector's art could be left for winter evenings when demands on time were not so hectic.

Plans were discussed for the next season at these times and the collection would be brought out and admired and the circumstances of many of the captures recited like Norse legends. This was the time, too, when Children's Hour demanded our attention, having been ignored during the long summer when the tempting outdoors took precedence. Cousin Loris, son of 'Aunty' Sheelagh and 'Uncle' Farquy, played the original Jennings on Children's Hour. They wanted me to have an audition too but to my aching dismay, Mum and Dad wouldn't allow it. The serial that still lives with me from those days was Masefield's 'Box of Delights', as true to the author and as full of wonder and adventure to our ears as anything I have encountered since. The Christmas Overture brings the whole thrill back whenever I hear it. Children's Hour was followed by the News with the impeccable voice of Stewart Hibberd or the more dramatic Frank Phillips reading it. They would always announce themselves at the start so you knew you weren't listening to Lord Haw Haw or some other impostor trying to put the wind up you. We did listen to him sometimes for laughs, with his 'Jairmany calling! Jairmany calling!' Nobody dared breathe during the News and it could have quite an influence on the atmosphere at bathtime. 'None of our aircraft failed to return' was greeted with cheers and we knew it would be a good night.

Winter was the time for long walks. It was almost a close season for gardening and, praise be, even logging, though there were large pieces in store which needed reducing to negotiable chunks. Tim and I would tackle the big stuff with the long cross-cut saw, a vicious length of naked blade with a vertical handle at each end. These were used by the professionals for felling trees locally and they would often lose their teeth (the saws, not the sawyers) on recently embedded shrapnel or long embedded cannon and musket shot, for the Battle of Britain was by no means the first to be waged over our fields. We would then split the sections with a heavy beetle and wedges – a satisfying job when a groaning oak log finally rent its knotted entrails and the rich smelling, salmon-pink wood was loaded on the forearms chin high to be stacked neatly in the inglenook baskets. Spuds had to be peeled, a daily chore, then lemonade at the Lion after a Saturday morning's work. After lunch we would stride out, with Dad setting a smart pace, our nailed boots crunching on the gravelled road.

Winter painted a broad landscape, when the trees and hedges lost their impenetrable screen and allowed sweeping views over hill and pasture and ploughland. Bare, red-brown earth with streaks of white, quiet now where so recently were the humming clover fields and whispering corn. Or stubble fields of short straw which rattled against your boots and sent chilly jets of water up the back of your legs after a night's rain. Partridges in their coveys sheltered in the stubble. Large flocks of tewits wintered on the plough – we always preferred the Yorkshire name. We never heard one say 'pee-wit' and though 'lapwing' was descriptive to a T, 'tewit' got our vote. On Robin Hill we would see wintering flocks of golden plover, so solitary in their northern nesting places, here in swift, elusive crowds, scarcely visible until they all banked together in flight, the sun briefly revealing the gold under each quick wing in a momentary flash. Here also we found thousands of small spiders on the move. Each would launch itself from a dry thistle head, paying out gossamer as the breeze caught it, repeating the process yards further on when it alighted again. The acres of pasture were covered in filamentous cobweb, parallel like the threads we strung to keep the sparrows off the peas.

One crackling, sparkling morning we woke to a silver thaw. I forget the intricate chain of conditions which must coincide to produce this miracle, as if the Snow Queen herself had passed over during the night, but the eerie beauty of the scene is deep engraved. We walked through a changed world. Dad told me that I may never see such a sight again in my life and would one day tell my grandchildren about it. He was right on the first count, though I love the story of the old countryman who, when asked if he had lived in the village all his life, cannily replied, 'Not yet!' Up to now I have no grandchildren. We walked up towards St John's and then swung right, through tiny hamlets with ancient names like Clay End and Slipe and

Bassus Green. Every twig, every leaf, every wisp of grass was encased in thinnest glass. Dried heads of cow parsley and the fruitless umbels of elder and the wayfaring tree shone in faceted crystal like chandeliers and in the stillness was the faintest tinkling as the grasses moved against each other, disturbed by startled birds. By mid day when the sun was up, it had gone. Perhaps all the most beautiful things have an evanescent quality inseparable from them.

Trudging home in a darkening world was the time for poetry. Dad had a capacious memory for his favourite poets and we absorbed poetry rather than learnt it, by far the best way. Milton had our countryside in mind when he wrote 'L'Allegro', and Gray must have been even better acquainted. There was the 'Rime of the Ancient Mariner', good for a mile or so, and for light relief we had the stirring ballads of Robert Service and the donnish laughter of Calverley, little remembered nowadays save for his stalwart 'Ode to Tobacco' embossed on the wall outside Bacon's in Cambridge. One wistful regular which always accompanied the final haul, past the six trees and over the brow when the Cottage would be in sight below and thoughts of log fires and tea and toast became almost a reality, was by Longfellow:

> I see the lights of the village
> Gleam through the rain and the mist,
> And a feeling of sadness comes o'er me
> That my soul cannot resist;
> A feeling of sadness and longing
> That is not akin to pain,
> And resembles sorrow only
> As the mist resembles the rain.

We had our own special pieces when called upon to recite, as children still were then. They were all long, which was one way of getting our own back. Tim went to excess by knowing the 'Elegy', all thirty-two stanzas. (Mind you, he was one of the only two friends I ever knew in later life who could accurately recite the entire saga of Eskimo Nell.) He would meander through it at parties at the drop of a hat. Mine was another of Gray's, the 'Ode on the Death of a Favourite Cat, Drowned in a Tub of Goldfishes'. I was tickled a year or two ago when Bernard Levin, a close friend of Tim later on and an eminent cat-man, in an article wrongly attributed my party piece to Oliver Goldsmith. I had a sneaking suspicion he and Gray could have been next door to each other in the *Dictionary of Quotations*. I wrote a splendid letter to *The Times*, full of wry comment and learned wit at the expense of my favourite columnist about my favourite cat, finishing 'nor all that glisters, Goldsmith!' which was a clever misquote from the very poem. They never printed it. Another of mine was 'Jonah and the Grampus', which I would only do wearing Dad's corduroy fishing jacket which reached down to my ankles and a grubby flat cap to match. I still do it sometimes though the cap is long lost. The fishing jacket only just reaches across my tummy. Tim and I painstakingly taught Patrick Browning's 'Home Thoughts from Abroad' and he coped superbly with one unsurmountable gap:

> . . . whoever wakes in England, sees some morning unaware
> That the lowest boughs and the brushwood sheaf
> Round the elm tree bole are in tiny leaf.

Patrick, now six, could never get his tongue round 'unaware'. The nearest we could steer him was 'ever air' and we had to be content with that.

Winter involved helping in the house on the distaff side, jobs which I never took to with much enthusiasm, but we were told on the authority of one of Mum's comics, *Woman's Journal* or *Good Housekeeping* or some such, that even the King helped with washing up in wartime and there were photographs to prove it. 'Don't you know there's a war on?' was a slogan which silenced grumbles, quelled mutiny and was generally used as an excuse for anything from the scarcity of beef to the unpunctuality of buses. Ethel oversaw our minor chores and organized us, friendly but firm, from getting up in the morning, scrubbed and combed, to teatime in the evening. Bathtime, storybook and bed were Mum's prerogatives. Ethel came to us when she was fourteen and remained throughout the war and after, with a brief absence when she was drafted into the munitions factory in Stevenage. She always great fun and part of the family. I don't think the title 'maid' was ever used – I suppose the modern 'mother's help' would be more appropriate. She lived with her family down Totts Lane in a friendly little cottage with no electric and no hot water, a fascinating patchwork of wallpaper culled from decorators' pattern books and a proud old wireless set with glass accumulator batteries which had to be taken up to Mr Boorman's the Cycle Shop to be recharged, When I was away at prep school, by prior arrangement Ethel would send me forged love letters to impress my friends, with loads of exclamation marks just like the real thing. 'I waited and waited by the stile for you on Thursday . . .!!!!!' I only had to say whether I wanted an angry one or a sloppy one. It was through Ethel that we became familiar with the pop songs of the day, for Bing Crosby and Vera Lynn produced the same reaction in Dad as the noisier stuff of today rouses in me though I show more tolerance. I think. Tim had the enviable ability to play any tune on the piano at first hearing, though he never learnt to read music properly – 'Don't Fence Me In' and 'All by Yourself in the Moonlight'. Good intellectual stuff!

Ethel's mother, the diminutive Mrs Parker, used to clean out the grates every morning with a brown pork-pie hat on her head, puffing like a little engine. Patrick would watch this with concentration. 'Porker! Why do you wear your hat in the house?' He had a gift for getting people's names slightly adrift with devastating effect. Mrs Parker was another loveable influence, brimful of warmth and fiercely devoted to Mum. Mum had Patrick's trick of getting phrases almost right, like 'Come on, we must all muckle down to it!' or 'Don't forget the Driver!' 'It's Diver, Mum! Oh really, Mum!' The catch phrase came from 'Itma' ('It's That Man Again!' Tommy Handley's archetypal radio comedy show) which we all adored and were allowed to come downstairs to listen to. That and 'Monday Night at Eight' which was my special privilege being the eldest. We eventually developed Mum's slight inaccuracies to a fine art. The best of the genre was Tim's rendering of President Lincoln's speech. It would start in ringing tones and falter to a hesitating climax. 'You can fool all the people some of the time, and some of the people all the time, but, er, you can't, um, fool all the people some of the time! . . . um.' We would roll about.

We used to go to London on occasions, to spend clothing coupons or to visit Mr Pitt, the dentist at Paddington Green. He would congratulate us on our teeth as though we had achieved something worthily Herculean, which took some of the anxiety out of it. Wartime London was coldly cheerless in winter, with no lights in shop windows and everyone looking rather drab as well they might. The pea soupers are a thing of the past but then they brought everything to a stop, though this included the Luftwaffe which was some consolation. The fog muffled all sound, even your own footsteps, claustrophobic, oily and yellow-green with a strange disinfectant smell. If you opened a door or window it would roll in like a viscous liquid, sluggishly inexorable, and the big stores became difficult to see across. I had a terror of being separated from the family and lost in the London fog. On these occasions we would take the train back from King's Cross and I would breathe again gladly when we could see the searchlights probing a clear sky.

Many fine winter afternoons were spent outdoors sketching with cartridge blocks and pencils. Trees and landscape, timbered and thatched cottages were taken in our stride, but Dad's forte was animals and birds. His technique was an effective one. We would find a field of calves or chickens, folds of sheep or a stable full of horses, and choose one individual as a subject to start. Nobody expects a hen to remain still for long, but once it had moved, you looked for another in the same position. Thus you could do detailed drawings of a series of composite hens, and the same with the calves and the rest. Patrick usually drew a hen 'doing an egg' and swore he saw it at the time. I have since used this method with guillemots and gannets and such where the trick pays rewarding dividends. We were also encouraged not to draw trees, but to draw oak trees or ash trees or elms or sycamores, for trees are as individual as animals, and unless you can feel the bark under your hands in your imagination, you are not competent to draw the tree from a distance. I soon learned each texture for it saved a lot of footwork. Pencils were of unpainted wood with WAR DRAWING stamped on them. I still have one. Five or Six Bs were lovely to draw and shade with but the devil to sharpen as the wood was as hard as the lead was soft and your pencil shrank rapidly.

Music was part of life though we preferred to make it rather than to listen to it. Dad found solace in his piano beyond the strife and the ever present danger in the operating theatres. However close the bombs, none of the team could cut and run with a patient on the table, and the strain must have often been hardly tolerable. I would wake to the sounds of Chopin, Liszt, Beethoven or Bach, depending on the mood, far into the night. Dr Stein would regularly come to stay for weekends and he and Dad would take turns accompanying each other on the violin. Dr Stein was a German Jew who had inadvertently escaped the Nazis by reading medicine at Cambridge. With the exception of a sister, also over here, his family were not so fortunate. He was not interned here, but was supposed to report to the local police station every evening. In fact, jovial Mr Berry would call in for a tankard or two and the law was duly observed in reverse as it were. Dr Stein was studying for his Fellowship, specializing in Ear, Nose and Throat, and Dad was coaching him. He was undeniably English to us, anyway, and later took out whatever papers made it official. He was an especial favourite of us three at Christmas and the only one of Dad's friends who ever helped with the washing up which raised his esteem in our eyes to a degree of partisanship. Tub drill was a bother and we welcomed all the help we could get.

Singing was as natural as breathing and I sang all the time. I must have had a fairly pleasing treble voice – I know it was a very loud one – but there were no tape recorders then, so I can only guess. Often I would be (willingly) brought down in my pyjamas into a haze of pipe and cigar smoke to join Dad at the piano in 'Wings of Song' or 'Haiden-Röslein' while pewter pots were quietly drained and refilled around me, until the voice of matriarchal authority packed me off upstairs again. The 'Erlking' would send us three into painfully suppressed hysterics, with its reference to 'nacht und wind' and 'es ist der Farter!' Joys were simple if rather crude. The German titles had an imagery lacking in the English. We always called the 'Joyful Peasant' the Frolicking Landman – my dear friend Dave and I used to play it as a duet for trombone and oboe. We had quite an orchestra among the Poetry Hailers once we reached our teens. I played the oboe, Dave the trombone and Jennifer the flute. Patrick scraped the 'cello and Sally a violin and Charles crooned down a clarinet and nearly everyone played the piano. Tim steadfastly refused all attempts to persuade him to take up an orchestral instrument, but sat in the kitchen area and played the triangle. So he had written for him a delightful concerto for solo triangle and orchestra called 'One Note of Love'.

Another winter thrill which I as the eldest was privileged sometimes to attend was pigeon shooting at night. A syndicate of farmers, Doc and 'Uncle' Bill Cox, the sexton, would have regular shoots in neighbouring woods and spinneys. It not only supplemented the meat ration, but helped to protect the winter crops like kale and sprouts which would be decimated by huge flocks of wood pigeons. The nightly habits of wood pigeons are fairly regular. They assemble in Wood A and roost in Wood B, and move severally from one to the other. In this instance they would gather in Sloggers Wood and fly in small parties to roost about two miles away in Box Wood, of Comma fame. Along the way they all stop in the same place to feed. We would wait for them in Box Wood until a sufficient number had arrived, then the whole party would let fly at once with both barrels. Of course it took ages for them to calm down and resettle. The same technique in Sloggers Wood produced the same panic. Now if one could only discover the spot where they all fed en route, then the pigeons could be potted in threes and fours without disturbing the rest yet to come in. After much careful search and observation, the secret was discovered, as with most important discoveries, by accident.

One day Bill Cox called in high excitement. In his official capacity he had been digging the grave of an old member of the syndicate, Alf Chalkley. Alf had been an amateur naturalist and the most skilful poacher in Hertfordshire. He and I used to be warily polite to each other among the shooting company, for I often used to go scrumping at the bottom of his orchard and he had known it. Once Mr Chalkley was up in Stevenage Court for shooting a pheasant on the wing. It was the same keeper who harassed us in the Little Woods. Old Alf arrived leaning on a white stick, wearing pebble spectacles, and had to be helped on to the stand. When the charge was read out and he was asked to comment, he said, 'Your Worship, I could'un shoot a pheasant if it were sitt'n in my lap!' The magistrate dismissed the case.

Bill reported that during his lugubrious excavations he had spotted the pigeons in the yews in the churchyard. 'There's a ready-made hide, Doc, I've just dug it, and the funeral's not till Monday. We can make a killing. Old Alf wouldn't 'alf chuckle!' Dad had visions of Monday's *Daily Mirror*: 'Harley Street Surgeon: Firearms in Fresh Dug Grave: Strange Rites Suspected'. He declined the invitation. The others risked the opprobrium from Press and Prelate and duly made their killing.

CHAPTER SEVEN

Unforgettable Yuletides

The Cottage

THE earlier wartime Christmases were very special. Nowadays Christmas and New Year punctuate the season before the long wait for spring, but one knows it will all be round again next year. Then we couldn't be so certain. A year is a long time when it represents some fifteen per cent of Life so Far, and there was the constant underlying fear that the war and family life and indeed Christmas itself could be lost before the next one had worked its way through. This very doubt made the festival a precious one and the friendly, 'all-in-it-together' atmosphere, so prevalent during the days of trial, was heightened at Christmas time.

Getting ready for Christmas started fairly early in that greetings had to be sent abroad to friends and relations in the services and those of the family still in India. These would take the form of airgraph letters. The original draft was on an official form rather larger than quarto size on which you wrote your letter and did your drawing, for no letter was complete without a drawing and with any luck you could get away with considerably more drawing than correspondence. Tim carried this into later life. At the height of his short career as illustrator and cartoonist, he would write to me with a letter head of gigantic size with some four lines of 'good, newsy letter' underneath. Our airgraphs would be photographed down to a small negative, flown out along with thousands of others, and enlarged the other end. Those coming to us in reply would be about five inches high and you had to read them with a magnifying glass.

We would get mysterious parcels which had to be hidden until Christmas. Tins of exotic sweets would come from Aunt Marjorie, Dad's sister in the Queen Alexandras who as a nursing officer followed the Eighth Army across the African desert, into Sicily, up through Italy and then crossed into Normandy in the wake of the liberating armies, finishing up in Germany itself. In 1945 King George decorated her with the Royal Red Cross, First Class. The sweet tins were sewn into canvas and stamped and censored and altogether looked as exciting as the contents. One, filled with Turkish Delight, arrived years late, battered out of shape, the ship having been sunk to the bottom of the Red Sea and the cargo later retrieved. The sweets were quite undamaged by their ordeal.

There were parties at our village school, and the inevitable village concert party to which we all walked, carrying our gas masks, with opaque blue paper pasted over our torches so that we could just see to tread safely without alerting enemy aircraft. Old friends and old protagonists in unfamiliar guises, singing popular songs, performing sketches and cracking jokes which we hardly understood but laughed loud with everybody else. 'Something About a Soldier' and 'When They Sound the Last All-Clear' and 'There'll Always Be an England!' But mostly Christmas was a family affair at home. The Cottage lent itself to Yuletide decoration like the traditional Christmas card with a robin in one corner and church bells in the other. The bells, of course, were silent throughout the land as they were reserved as an alarm in the event of the invasion. The ropes in the church tower were hoisted high out of reach where they hung in an intriguing parabola with their gaily coloured woolly lagging visible over the carved oak screen at the back of the aisle. Mr Bayes the butcher had given us a treasure chest of old, pre-war tinsel and trimmings to which we added our own laboriously made paper streamers and Chinese lanterns. Precious baubles and tree lights were handled with care and unwrapped from orange papers and later packed away again cautiously for who knew when one would be able to buy such things again? The predominating motif was of holly, ivy and mistletoe culled from the trees and hedges and nailed on to the interlacing oak beams as though they had grown there all the year round. A huge oak Yule log burned for days on the dogs in the inglenook, surrounded by smaller satellites of hornbeam which, when the bark was off, were delicately fluted like Edinburgh Rock. We felt a glow from the products of our labours in the woods which was not entirely due to the sparks and the blaze.

We had a house full for the Christmas of 1942 – there were Mum's brothers, Uncle Arthur, who had got his wings, and Uncle John, who was a Desert Rat, and a New Zealander friend of his with an enormous moustache like a shoe brush, known simply as 'Whit'. By the next Christmas all three were dead. I often reflect with something of a shock that I am the longest surviving male scion of the Edwards family for many generations. They were all killed in wars. My maternal grandfather, a doctor, was killed in 1917 when my mother was only ten. He never saw Arthur, his youngest. My grandmother, she of the black hair and blue eyes, died shortly afterwards, it was said of a broken heart. Arthur's eldest daughter was there at the Cottage as a baby that Christmas. He in his turn never met his youngest.

Arthur was a remarkable man – though I realize now he would only have been in his early twenties at the time. We loved to hear stories about him for he had been a notorious scapegrace as a small boy. When Great Aunt Alice (a Queen Victoria in stature, with much of the same unbending authority, who numbered Kipling among her friends and wrote for Chambers' *Journal*), had visited Eastbourne on one of her rare trips from India, Arthur had surpassed himself by borrowing his brother John's cornet and playing 'Alice, Where Art Thou?' in the square gardens outside, early in the morning of her first day. They removed his bathing costume as a punishment for this, but had to return it as he simply put to sea in the buff – a far greater crime than one can imagine today, and fraught with dire consequences. He had an amazing way with horses. They would trot up to him from far across a field as though they had known him all their lives. Even the Hitler horse in 'The Walks', a grey, grumpy old carthorse with a shock of black forelock sweeping diagonally across his brow like Adolf's, who would normally follow us menacingly with his lips drawn back over his teeth, came up to Uncle Arthur and nuzzled him like a lamb. He had gone to Officer Training School before the outbreak of war, intending to be a pilot, but his salad days had produced more success on the games field than in the examination hall and he had to retake all his School Certificate maths and science. Eventually they failed him. Little daunted, he decided to join up in the ranks and get there the long way. He found that many families with whom he had been a welcome guest as an officer cadet now closed their doors to him as a mere private. After some time spent as a rear gunner, he finally achieved his ambition for a few crowded hours of glorious life.

Uncle John was older, less flamboyant, thoughtful and quiet, with a love of the countryside and our family life which impressed itself on me though he never spoke of it. He spoke of much pain and weariness though, in isolation, for to talk to small boys must have been like talking to himself – they trotted alongside like spaniels and seemed to take as little heed. He had been farming successfully in New Zealand when he had joined up and was on leave from North Africa on this, his last visit. He had met 'Monty' and was full of enthusiasm for the uncompromising attitude of their new commander of the Eighth Army. The tide had started to turn against Rommel and the battle in Egypt had been successful, later to be known as the Battle of Alamein. The New Zealanders had been taken out of the line temporarily, after heavy fighting, and John and his friend, Whit, had managed to wangle a brief Christmas leave. After he had gone back the newspapers announced that we had captured Rommel's scarf. I sent Uncle John a drawing of a crocodile with a scarf in its mouth, labelled '8th Army', chasing Rommel as Hook. He must have enjoyed it as it was returned with his effects, a fading airgraph letter. The church bells were indeed to ring again, the next May, in celebration of the final victory in Tunisia, but by that time John and Whit could no longer hear them.

That Christmas dinner was hardly typical of the time. We had a turkey of our own, another as a present from one of the hospitals, and a goose from Yorkshire where they were convinced we were having to eat hay. We were on strict orders not to talk of this at school as so many children would not be so lucky as ourselves. In truth such an injunction was quite unnecessary as we had a horror of being smeared with a 'black market' label. This stigma had taken over from the spy category as the ultimate brand of Cain and phrases like 'under the counter' and 'forged points' were bandied about in undertones. The postmistress, who treated the war as a personal affront, kept sweets 'under the counter' for 'her' children, by which she meant bona fide villagers, not evacuees or upstart newcomers like us. Your sweets were strictly on ration anyway, but supplies would often fall short of demand. You never saw sweets for sale in the post office, though forlorn jars labelled Bull's Eyes and Barley Sugar stood around on shelves waiting for better days. I met the real black market at Kilnsey Show, or so I thought. A Wharfedale farmer friend had won the first prize for a monstrous ham. In the tent, Dad congratulated him.

'It would be a shame if that were to go off, wouldn't it!'

'Canst think on a way o' stoppin' it, Sam?'

No more was said, but when we left, the ham lay under a sack in the car boot. I was convinced that armed police would get us all the way home.

Our Christmas pudding was from Grannie who always made hers years in advance to mature and had a supply of pudding which outlasted the war. 'Aunt' West was there, of course – she spent every Christmas with us – and she underwent much teasing as she had solemnly boiled the sixpences in the sterilizer before inserting them to be boiled in the pudding. Loud rang the choruses round the piano, carol after carol, 'A Great Big Shame' and 'The 'Ouses in Between' and 'The Miner's Dream of Home'. The wireless struck more solemn notes with a talk from Mr Churchill and the one from the King when, as always, people said how marvellous he was to do it with his stammer. I was never aware of his stammer, though he gave long, dramatic pauses which made his speech all the more impressive. Tuning in was quite a business. There was the Home Service and the Forces' Programme and strange stations like Antwerp and Hilversum which produced nothing but a loud Swanee whistle. We had a traditional story, originating from Gramp, about the time that the King went to Dad for a consultation. The routine went as follows:

> King: Hallo, Sam!
> Sam: Hallo, King! What's to do?
> King: Sam, I think there's summat wrong wi' this ear.
> Sam: This 'ere wot, King?

It ran on in this vein for some time. They never did meet, Sam and t'King, but other members of the family were among his patients. Dad never knew how important to us some of his patients were – he never went to the cinema and rarely listened to the wireless – though he did get us Basil Radford's autograph. He performed a mastoidectomy on him and whenever we saw the lovable Blimp on the screen alongside Naunton Wayne, we would point proprietorially to the scar and tell friends with pride, 'Our Dad did that!' Jack Hulbert used to sit on the table in the Waiting Room, sacrilegiously swinging his legs and making cracks and would swear it was his most frosty audience. Dad wanted to straighten out his enormously displaced nasal septum. Would it improve his nose and his speaking voice? Dad fell into the trap and assured him it would. 'Then you keep your hands off it,' he was told, 'they're worth a fortune to me!' Dad's first private operation had been on old Vivian van Damm of the Windmill, and Mum got her first fur coat.

London produced its pantomimes even in those dark days and what spectacular treats they were! In 1942 we went to Cinderella at His Majesty's, with Bobby Howes as an endearing Buttons and Evelyn Laye as Prince Charming. Patrick found his way on to the stage, whether or not by invitation I can't remember, and was picked up and given a big kiss by Miss Laye, amid shouts from two boxes full of pilot officers who all wanted one too. The following Christmas I achieved a lifetime ambition and we went to Peter Pan at the Cambridge Theatre. Ann Todd was Peter and Alastair Sim did the traditional double as Mr

Darling and Hook and the results were sheer magic. I fell desperately in love with Joyce Redman as Wendy. She never knew. The play was played as a play and taken seriously as such or I couldn't have borne it. I have seen it in later years produced as the corniest panto by people who should have known better, and have left, sick and fuming, in the middle of it. Once again, I believe, the wheel has turned fullest of circles and Peter is being played, as he should be, by a young man. I have great faith in a Barrie revival before long. On my eleventh birthday I was given his complete works, at my request, and found my way through all the fantasy and all the islands from start to finish, spellbound and uncritical. I had produced two acts of Peter myself before that, at school, with relative success – the Home Underground and the Pirate Ship, for they didn't involve flying. Even my inventive aspiring couldn't rise to that. It still didn't get him out of my system, and nothing ever has.

The next Christmas, 1944, was to be the last of the war and it snowed. By this time we were away in the North at prep school and decorating started directly we got home for the holidays. Patrick almost hid the loo in intricate webs of paper chains and early in the morning we were out for holly. Mediterranean convoys had become safe and the cousins and aunts arrived in a body from India. There were Mum's sister, Maisie, her three sons, Edward and David and baby Michael who was born just before they left India, and Great Aunt Ethel, Mum and Maisie's aunt, who was voluminous and rather vague and altogether delightful. The boys had never seen it snowing before and indeed had never been so cold and yellow, like Mary in *The Secret Garden*, but we had enormous fun.

Later Christmases became increasingly heavy with responsibility for me – I acquired jobs like supervising the fuel or plucking the bird or, heaven help us, icing the cake, but in 1944 I was untrammelled and without a care except for the spud bashing and tub drill which we all had to share. I shudder at icing the cake; Tim and I used to go to lengths of surrealism that Dali himself might have envied. It would start conventionally enough, with holly and mistletoe designs round the edge, but would soon acquire dotted lines and scissors saying 'cut here' and protruding arms and little balloons saying 'Help! Let me out!' One year we produced a snowy roof with a chimney in the middle. Up one side of the gable were neatly sculped footprints leading to the chimney. On the other side were black bootmarks weaving unsteadily down again to the guttering. We kept these a great secret until the actual day or they would probably have been banned. One of Tim's cards I treasure graphically depicts a Santa with a Machiavellian grin, a smoking rifle in his hand and a dead reindeer at his feet. It wasn't that Tim didn't love Christmas – he just hated being expected to.

A festivity which started in the war years and became quite an institution in the village was our New Year's Eve fancy dress party where we toasted the New Year in at nine o'clock in cider. Children would start asking Mum about it around September and would their little brother be old enough to come this year? In the first one Tim made a stunning Bo-Peep with crinoline and petticoats devised from pre-war evening dresses long out of service and cardboard bonnet and ribboned crook. 'Uncle' Len, always ready with an apposite quote from the 'Halls', sang, 'Coom, pretty one, coom, coom, coom, coom!' whereupon the disgruntled shepherdess pulled the customary faces and flounced off to get dressed as a pirate. Dr Stein was always recruited as a convincing Father Christmas and the Rector would look in, wearing an impossible false beard and fool nobody. Around eight o'clock would come an urgent telephone call for Dad and he would hastily disappear in the car while 'Uncle' Len's womenfolk, 'Aunty' Beet and 'Aunty' Ethel, would cluck in sympathy for the poor Doctor whose time was never his own. I later found out the emergency took the form of a vacant hand at crib at the White Lion – I had wondered about the regularity with which patients would take a turn for the worse during the annual fancy dress party.

Charades were an essential part of the entertainment and we cheated shamelessly. 'Granulated' came up once, as in sugar. How the syllables were enacted, I forget, but the final word was represented by a gruesome emergency appendicectomy in the family kitchen: 'Gran, you lay Ted on the table and I'll sharpen the bread knife!' When everybody had gone and we were ready for bed, we were allowed down to the inglenook for Ghost Stories and Pictures-in-the-Fire. Our own domestic wraiths were summoned and many local ones and authorities like M. R. James and Algernon Blackwood were called into service. Our village was in fact the residence of the last wretch to be arraigned as a witch, one Jane Wenham, early in the eighteenth Century. She had all the hallmarks. They could stick pins in her and she bled not, nor showed signs of pain. She couldn't repeat the Lord's Prayer without mistakes and cats 'were wont to lurk in her presence in a most peculiar manner'. She should have had a jackdaw, but no doubt that would have been held against her as well. The poor Jane was sentenced to death at Hertford, but the judge got her pardoned and she finished her days in peace on his estate. We had a witch in the village even then, Little Old Mary, once, incredibly, the light o'love of the landlord of the White Lion. She was hunched up double with a chin and nose that met like Mr Punch and wore flapping black and had pointed boots with turned-up toes. She grew the best vegetables in the village which she sold from a basket – huge clean carrots and parsnips and tight, crisp cabbages. But it was rumoured that she raised them with 'night soil' and only the very poor people would buy them. Nowadays they would be called 'organic' and only the very rich people would afford them. Another bogeyman was Luffenhall Jack, the frog man, though we found he was really rather simple and cautiously friendly. He had webbed fingers and lived up the chalk Roman Road beyond White Hill where we would pass his lonely garden on butterflying expeditions. He tended his vegetables as his family must have done for centuries, digging with a tined branch like an antler and flattening the soil with boards strapped to his feet.

Singing in the choir involved Midnight Mass on Christmas Eve, cassocked and surpliced, and I would often read one of the Nine Lessons. The hour and the musty scents and the candlelight and the haunting carols combined to make this a wonderful overture to the fun in store. Ours was a pretty church, of Norman flint and very old in parts, though not so immediately picturesque as some. We always looked in at the churches when our rambles took us to neighbouring villages. Ardeley, a mile and a half away, was almost too 'Merrie England' to be true. In fact I don't think it was as 'olde' as it looked. The church, opposite the green and a semi-circle of much too perfect white walled thatched cottages, was undoubtedly genuine. It boasted a lych gate with a porch which ours did not. The roof was full of carved wooden angels playing musical instruments, and I envied the choirboys with so much to hold their attention during the sermons.

Our church required closer inspection for real interest, as one soon tired of deciphering the stones and memorial plaques to long departed Humberstones and Gorsuches with their puzzling 'facreds' and 'iffues' and 'refurrections'. One had to rely on the bats and intruding birds to provide diversion through the fidgety address. Out of hours when the church was empty we browsed much, more to search for moths on the sills of the stained-glass windows, which often yielded a prize or two, than because of any passion for history and architecture. But we absorbed the latter along with everything else which was all grist to our mill. There was a fine stone crusader in armour, a Knight Templar, lying cross-legged with his spurs on and a shield in his left hand, just like the one Bernard Miles used to talk about when he and his mates would climb in through the vestry window and sharpen their scythes and fangin' hooks on him. 'Best bit of sharpenin' stone in 'Ertfordshire! 'Is Old Woman ain't no good though. Can't get a good edge on 'er!' A stone with brass figures inlaid recalled William Chapman, Citizen and Haberdasher of London, and we wondered if he had arrived full tilt like John Gilpin who only got as far as Ware, about seven miles short of us. Below the brass William and his wife were their six sons and their six daughters, all kneeling and uniformly alike. One of the Humberstones 'had two wives', although it didn't say whether he had them one at a time or both at once. The nicest was erected to her husband by a Mary Humberstone in, I think, 1627. She waxed poetic:

> 'Tis not a Stone, dear Sir, can deck your Herse,
> Nor can your worth lodge in a narrow Verse.

She was determined to have a bash, whatever. She ended up, as I recall, saying that the monument, showing herself and her man sitting at a desk reading, was . . .

> Erected by the ingenious trust
> Of a sad wife in honour of your dust.

Touching, that, we felt, though possibly a bit flowery. Naturally we had great fun composing our own valedictory rhymes:

> Beneath this stone lies James.
> He had a lot of ruder names.

There was no serviceable rhyme to Patrick except hat trick which had a sporty ring but lacked the right funereal flavour.

> Here lies Tim.
> People were quite fond of him.

Modest as always. One intriguing stone in the graveyard was tiny and of great age. It was undated and simply said, leaving worlds of speculation, 'Here lyeth the body of Cock'. Tim rests there now. I never had the heart to suggest his own epitaph.

The churchyard, enclosed by an old flint wall, was fringed with lime trees and, in true Gray's Elegy fashion, the heaving turf was overshadowed with rugged elms and yew trees. There was even a moping barn owl in the belfry who gave us a tremendous scare once when we were night mothing. We were told that the yews were grown in the churchyard to provide wood for the longbows many wars ago. The berries and the bark are poisonous and it was the one place where the cattle had no access. Next to it the River Beane formed a pool when it was in working order and flowed over the lane where there was a ford and another little hand bridge. Here there was often a kingfisher which sped away like a blue spark when you disturbed it, and we once watched a family of water shrews, black coated and white tummied like tiny penguins, which turned to quicksilver in the water like the diving beetles. A private bridge above the pool led through gardens to the Old Rectory, erected by the son of the same Daniel Gorsuch, Citizen and Mercer of London, whose monument afforded me my idle reading from the choir stalls. He, the son, was the rector in 1632 and built 'a Square Pile of Brick' which was later taken from the family for their loyalty to King Charles. No Vicar of Bray, he! Our rector, Dr Greenham, lived in a more modern and more modest house nearby, but the lovely old square pile of brick remained, with a finely proportioned cedar tree on the lawn and tall beeches and horse chestnuts where noisy generations of rooks brought up their annual broods.

In this spacious garden were held the village fêtes during 'Wings for Victory' week and other fund-raising occasions for the war effort. A five-foot bomb was labelled 'A Present to Hitler' and we bought savings stamps and stuck them on the surface till all the metal was hidden. We were assured that it would be straightway filled with explosive and dropped over Berlin. I borrowed Ethel's shoes and came runner-up in an ankle competition, standing behind a sight screen from the cricket field. The competitors enjoyed the joke but the judge seemed a bit surprised. There were other pastimes such as the greasy pole, knocking a chap's topper off as he walked up and down behind a screen, and a half-crown at the bottom of a bucket of water. You paid a penny and put your hand in, but the bucket had a static charge which made your hand clench tighter the deeper you went, and before you reached the half-crown you couldn't open it. The Infants' Class presented a circus, with the local villain, who looked set to follow Mr Chalkley as premier of the poachers even at his tender years, cracking the whip as ringmaster and improving his image in the process for he was somewhat notorious. Patrick was cast as the back end of the elephant and won popular, though necessarily shared, acclaim. I have always felt it was one of his most sensitive portrayals of a role.

CHAPTER EIGHT

Hails and Farewells

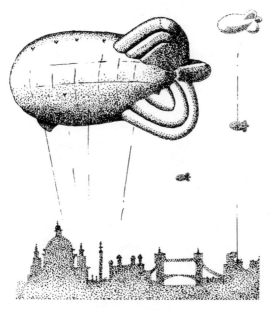

Barrage balloons

EARLY in the summer of 1944 we met our first American airman. One sunny afternoon, just as we were due to be dismissed from school for the day, a Flying Fortress laboured into view, flying low over Robin Hill, just visible over the top of Dick Foster's farm and the cider brewery. The noise drowned the hymn and we watched agog as a cluster of olive and brown parachutes blossomed from the huge plane which went on, sinking, northwards. Tim and I had taken a rough guess at where the parachutes should come down and raced homewards, turning left up Froghall Lane before we reached our Cottage. On we panted up the familiar cart track to which the lane soon gave way and in a cornfield just short of Box Wood we found our American, swearing profusely and struggling with his parachute. On seeing us he lumbered over the ditch and on to the path and sat down, a boy on either side. He was overdressed for warm weather. From the depths of a sort of haversack he brought chocolate and chewing gum and we sat there, me, typically, overcome with shyness and Tim chatting away brightly. We had never met chewing gum before either, and I didn't like it much. Our new friend kept his jaws moving in a rotary motion like a companionable cow. After a while he said he guessed we'd better take him to the police station. It seemed a bit harsh as he hadn't really done anything but trample a bit of corn and nobody could think he was a spy. We told him there wasn't one but we could take him to Mr Berry's house and he was the policeman.

When we got back to the post office at the bottom of Froghall Lane, there was Mr Berry himself, a few Military Policeman with a jeep and a handful of other sweating airmen each with their escort of children who had done as we had and raced off to the rescue. Only one young felon, the erstwhile ringmaster of the garden fête, had shot off on his bike beyond the top end of the village and found the crashed Fortress. Down the High Street he sailed, his brakes woefully ineffective, swathed and counter-crossed with belts of live ammunition like a Mexican bandit. An astonished MP grabbed him as he fell off his bike scattering shells all over the road. Mercifully nothing went off.

Around this time, upheavals took place in the established order of things which I found unsettling and in some cases very sad. The war seemed to be receding. The searchlight battery had packed up and the soldiers had gone, leaving the barrack huts all empty. The perpetual convoys no longer wound through the lanes and the khaki trucks and the waving men, once so much a part of the shifting scene, had passed by for the last time. As Tim and I had been at our Stevenage private school to start with, we had not seen the arrival of the evacuees at the local village school. Now the evacuees were beginning to return home and I realized that I didn't really know who was a permanent fixture and who was not, as they had become so integrated into our lives. Many of my indigenous friends had deliciously rustic nicknames which could have inspired a Samuel Beckett, like 'Prunger' and 'Bullney' and 'Gudgin' but even this was not a certain guide, and from Christmas on I witnessed with dismay many firm-founded friendships dissolve as the boys and one or two girls, with whom I had grown up, unexpectedly left us and went back to London or wherever.

Early in the morning of June 6th we were awakened by a noise unlike anything we had ever heard before, familiar though we were with the nightly roar of bombers setting off for the Continent and returning in early daylight. We rushed outside. The sky from horizon to horizon was full of aircraft heading south in formation; everywhere you looked a mass of relentless planes, grimly purposeful, utterly invincible. For the first time ever I felt a joyful conviction that no way could we lose the war. 'The sixth hour of the sixth day of the sixth month!', shouted Tim above the din, and it sounded convincing. For this at last was 'D-Day', a term used for any operation, but now exclusively associated with the Normandy invasions. Not till long after did we realize this timing was mere coincidence and the invasion had been postponed for two or three anxious days due to bad weather. All the planes we knew were there and in those days I recognized everything that flew (today I couldn't name you one unless it be a historical relic in a ceremonial fly-past). Huge Halifax and Stirling Bombers towing gliders, Lancasters, Flying Fortresses and the twin-engined Marauders, Dakotas with their back-swept wings, nifty Spitfires and Hurricanes and their American rivals, the Mustangs and the Thunderbolts, the strange, twin-bodied Lightnings like aerial Catamarans and, far above them all, the triangular wings of the little Mosquitoes, like cocktail glasses in silhouette. Planes on planes, from the nearby airfields of Cambridgeshire and Suffolk and others from further north, all moving inexorably south, their places in the sky ever taken by others as they melted into the distant horizon above High Wood.

It was the spectacle of a lifetime – indeed I trust it will never be seen again in any lifetime – but it stirred the blood to shouting excitement and we cheered ourselves hoarse. Rome had fallen, I think the day before, and we had rejoiced at that and on the news at breakfast time we were told that the Navy and the Air Force had begun to land the Allied armies on the coast of France. Subsequent news was a bit of an anticlimax – even Richard Dimbleby broadcasting from a Halifax taking a troop glider in, a shade more excitable than his later epics smoothly reporting royal wedding and coronation, or Wynford Vaughan Thomas shouting from a track in Normandy above the rattle of passing tanks. While the planes were overhead we felt we were part of it. Now it was back to sticking flags vicariously in the map and listening to the wireless.

Such detachment was illusory. Only about a week after this, Tim and I were staying overnight with Dad in the flat in Harley Street. Once again we were wakened in bed by a loud roar as of a squadron of bombers overhead. This time the noise stopped abruptly and we were jolted by a shattering explosion. Air raids had become a bad memory and London was supposed to be safe now. Dad came in quickly to reassure us and as the raid seemed to be over we eventually settled down again. The next day the rumours were rife and we learned that what we had heard was Hitler's long threatened secret weapon, a V1 Flying Bomb, which had exploded about two miles away at Bethnal Green, killing I think nine people. The noise made by a single Doodlebug, as they came to be called, was deafening, like a dozen Spitfires at full throttle. This had been the first night of the Doodlebugs and proved to be our last night in London for nearly a year to come.

That we became fairly familiar with these indiscriminate destroyers shows how inaccurate their target settings must have been, either, as it was rumoured, due to Resistance sabotage or simply because the launching grounds were being overwhelmed before the weapons had been perfected and they were fired off hurriedly in a hit-or-miss fashion. Certainly many of them missed, landing harmlessly in fields. The Mosquitoes became adept at shooting them down and we cheered at one, probably apocryphal, account of one of these plywood heroes which actually managed to turn a Doodlebug round over the Channel and send it back the way it came. It was easy to be valiant when out of danger and such stories were good for morale, but with their squat wings and the elongated megaphone above the tail, these mindless robots were truly frightening. We would see them occasionally speeding in a dead straight line when we were butterflying in the clover fields, and they bred a helpless fear. If the noise cut out you threw yourself face down on the ground with one hand over your nose and mouth and the other pressed into your tummy to prevent the blast from forcing in through your lungs and blowing your insides out. A slow count of fifteen and you heard the colossal bang. Then you would rush home to find out where it had landed. At night all you could see was the fiery blast of the exhaust pluming out behind it. We never had one very near but for me these were the nastiest moments of the whole war.

The V2s were much deadlier, but as they travelled faster than sound you heard the bang first and then the screeching crescendo, like the last screaming defiance of the demented Führer, as they came down. The neighbouring tiny village of Aston, two and a half miles away, was half destroyed by one of these. Somehow they were less frightening, for if you heard the explosion you knew it hadn't got you. Their heyday was mercifully short. If the Nazis had had time to perfect these rockets and pinpoint them accurately, the story could have been very different. As it was, over 2,000 flying bombs landed on London alone and I believe some 9,000 people were killed and 25,000 injured before the raids stopped abruptly at the end of the following March.

Things were beginning to get rough again on the home front and in September, just after the V2s began to be a menace, a long talked of conscription became a reality and we were all three packed away to prep school in Yorkshire to be near Grannie and Gramp. In retrospect it seems that the Normandy invasion and the subsequent liberation were no more than a prolonged mopping up operation but the reality was nothing like so optimistic. Disasters like Arnhem were to follow, and the Ardennes, and the outcome of the war still hung in the balance for all we knew. Only recently I inherited Gramp's life-long amassed stock of fly-tying paraphernalia, much of it in the old chest with some fifty tiny drawers which used to stand in his optician's workshop when I was a child. It dates back in fact to the jewellers and clockmakers of a generation before. In one of the drawers lay hidden, under feathers and tinsel, a collection of letters written to him by Dad at the time of which I am speaking. Extracts show that the terror was far from over:

10, Harley Street, W.   13/11/44

Dear Dad,

Just a scribbled line – I have no time to myself at all. It is now 11.15 (pm). I was operating until 8.0 and got here at 10.0 and have been on the phone ever since. It is very hard to cope with it all – we have been having V2s etc which have up-ended life again. I have just heard that my usual route to Woolwich tomorrow has been quite liquidated so I shall have to go to New Cross and then find out the way. This will add half-an-hour or so to a programme that already takes me till 8.0 or 8.30 pm. But there you are – this is London life! . . . A call has come through about a chap whose nose has started to bleed after a V2 'incident' in Bexley Heath, so I have had him taken to Woolwich where KRO will look after him until I arrive tomorrow. I saw a girl today who was flung on to a gas stove by blast and lay there for three hours – slowly cooking. She is alive, but it is difficult to see how she will ever again be a human individual. These things produce hundreds of dead as there is no warning at all. One fell in Petticoat Lane at 1.45 pm on Friday – you can imagine the casualty list if you know the district! There were 60 casualties brought to Barts, and I expect the London Hosp wd. have an equal number. I was at Barts at the time and we even heard it – but I was working & I don't think I wd. hear even the Crack of Doom if I were on a job
. . .

10, Harley Street, W.   9/3/45

Dear Dad,

Sorry I have not had time to write, but I hardly have time even to 'go out to t'back' these days, and that's just the trouble, as Tim would say. The rockets are getting to be more than somewhat of a nuisance. We had three near misses at Woolwich on Tuesday and on Wed. morning I was doing a mastoid at Woolwich when a large piece of rocket fell on the roof, but did not seep through. I then went to Victoria Park through scenes suggesting a recent earthquake, and was operating there only to have all the dummy windows blown in – thank goodness they were cellophane, not glass. I am still timing my movements very cleverly, because I was ½hr. late for Barts today, and one landed in Farringdon Street just where I cross in my car, ½hr. before I arrived. Barts' windows are all out again and we are crammed with casualties. The thing fell at 11.30 and you know what the population of Farringdon Street is at 11.30 am. The death roll must be terrible. BANG – one has just gone off outside – I wonder where? Pretty close – maybe about Oxford St. Shall be glad to get home tomorrow night. Ambulance bells just starting to ring – so it must be nearish. Poor old London is getting very tattered – I hope it won't be long now. Keep smiling,

Sam

P.S. If owt happened, you'd look after the lads, wouldn't you?

10, Harley Street, W.   14/3/45

. . .We have mercifully been fairly quiet so far this week. There was only one rocket last night, nearish but not too near, and 2 flying bombs. Our wards are still full of casualties. The little mangled babies with their troubled eyes are hard to see and keep the lump out of one's throat. Last Thursday's V2 in Smithfield was bad. We had 328 casualties at Barts., 122 serious. There were 50 dead and the roll is increasing – now over 100 and still many under the ruins. We lost 2 nurses and another has lost a leg. Last Wed. I was held up in Blackwall Tunnel for 30 mins. in a traffic jam. A rocket fell on the Poplar end just 15 mins. after I got through on my way to Victoria Park. I came that way today and thanked the Lord when I saw what I had missed by 10 mins. There is very little left of East London now. I have 3 or 4 private cases next month – confidence is returning. I only need *peace* to make good financially. I know I am making good in God's sight – if work and love are the requisites.

God bless you,
Sam

135

I was frightened for my parents and leaving home and privacy for a strange new community life was an uncomfortable uprooting, but my chief regret was leaving the butterflies. We knew of old that Yorkshire was miserly when it came to insect life. Oddly enough, when I moved even further north to public school at Sedbergh, I found a comparative abundance of butterflies and moths, but for some reason, whether ancient and glacial or modern and industrial, the more southerly of the Yorkshire Dales have a scant population. Malsis Hall had some sixty boys, presided over by Bernard Gadney, last and biggest of the big English scrum halves and one of the last and biggest of the big English headmasters. He had revived Malsis from the days when there were too few boys to constitute a XV, let alone a 1st XV, and he and his dear wife, Kelly, were to prove staunch friends to me for many years to come. At the time, Bernard was in the Royal Navy, his post being filled by a deputy, and would appear on leave hugely resplendent with gold rings on his jacket. At ten I was rather older than the average new boy and Patrick, at six, was considerably younger, but as there were three of us and in view of the hazards in the south, he was welcomed as part of the job lot and treated like a sort of mascot. He became a professional 'Youngest Boy of the School' for nearly two years, always in demand by visiting conjurors. Reggie, then the sole son and heir to the Gadneys, was slightly younger, though not officially 'at the school' so somehow he didn't count as the youngest. How the two of them passed their days, I never knew, struggling as I was for the first time with Latin declensions and French verbs, but I don't think it was with anything too strenuously academic, most of it involving a huge wooden railway engine on the cricket field. School uniforms were things of the past due to clothes rationing, and we three wore corduroy lumber jackets in our habitual colours. I think it was the only way they told us apart.

My first impression of Malsis was of swarms of model aeroplanes. Many beautifully made, they were suspended all over from the ceilings of classrooms and dormitories, British and American planes facing one way, enemy planes the other. Plane modelling was by far the most popular hobby. The kits were of the simplest, not the intricate ready-made plastic jigsaws that are assembled today. You started by transferring plans on to a block of hard wood and set to work with a penknife and sandpaper. The classrooms reeked of 'dope' and balsa cement and judging by the reported effects of 'solvent abuse' today, we must all have been on a permanent high. Letters home were mandatory every Sunday and Mum would write every week and send us a copy of the Mickey Mouse comic. Dad would write to me on rare occasions, usually in Latin which I was learning to love. 'Me care Jacobe . . .' Enjoying Latin was something I learned to keep quiet about, along with 'bughunting', as the eccentric was frowned on until he became established, whereupon he was in danger of becoming a poseur. My ability to draw helped my social standing and I found we had a sort of kudos from being of the small group of 'London Boys', coming as we did from the thick of it and with some good stories to tell. Certainly we were specially looked after in small ways by the Gadneys, particularly by Bernard's mother, Old Mrs G., who presided over the cocoa trolleys and had us to tea on special occasions.

Diet seems, in retrospect, to have consisted entirely of tinned herrings and prunes, neither of which I have been able to stomach since. The amount of butter/margarine mixture (it went further that way) that you might nowadays put on your potatoes at a sitting, was your ration for the week. After that it was dry bread. An ingenious friend called Ian Smith – a lady's man of eleven years who was most impressed by Ethel's 'love letters' – decided to make his own butter to supplement the ration. Soon we were all at it. Little bottles filled with milk were strapped to the calf under the sock and we swung our legs throughout lessons, under the desks, until we achieved a sort of curds and whey. Then salt was added. I suppose we ate the results, I don't remember. At home most of the milk had been of the powdered variety, even though dairy herds munched all round us, especially the American tins of Klim (milk spelt backwards of course) which we got through Paddington Green. Here fresh milk was in fair supply as Bernard ran the school farm with a small herd. Sometimes they got on to the beck side among the wild garlic. The stench from the milk was appalling but it was all we had to drink. Didn't we know there was a war on?

In the Dales, grazing land was ploughed up to grow wheat and oats, but, coming from lush arable land myself, I could see that the efforts were hardly worth the trouble for the reluctant, straggled crops that resulted. At Malsis, 'Digging for Victory' was taken seriously. Most of the nine-hole golf course, pride of the Old Boys in the weak piping time of peace, had been ploughed up and we grew potatoes and turnips and all took a hand in the harvesting. The dairy herd grazed on what was left. The games fields were largely uncut and grew hay for winter feed once the rugger season was over. Haymaking was a splendid alternative to lessons in the late summer term. The cricket square was sacrosanct, for there were some institutions which had to withstand Hitler or our island would be lost, but even the summer house by the ornamental lake was barred and boarded with a sign saying 'Danger – Explosives!' Ancient trees were culled along the drive for fuel. A sudden roll-call, like a surprise *appel* in a P.O.W. camp, once gave us alarm. A tree had been felled across the drive leaving a small boy standing upright among the branches once it had settled. Everyone was present. Bernard after a whispered consultation apologized. The offending survivor had been his son, Reg, who had been watching the work to its dramatic conclusion. Had the tree shifted a foot or so either way, the populace would have been denied a handful of best-selling thrillers, two sensitive television plays and some masterly work on Constable which I keep on the table in my study.

Over and above the school on the moor was a square tower, memorial to the wife of the wool baron who had first built the fine old square, Georgian-style house, before it was later embellished with porch and parapets and its own tower of Victorian Baroque. Gramp was a keen amateur astronomer and would train his powerful telescope on the moor-top tower from Skipton, several miles away, when we warned him we were going up there on an expedition. We would hold up messages and it was most exciting when he would read them back to us later. He was in the Home Guard, a Sergeant, and spent many nights a week safeguarding our homes in a little hut way on the top of Crookrise, by playing poker and dominoes with his mates.

There was an observation post below the boundary obelisk which balanced the square tower at the other end of the moor above. Here the member of the Observer Corps who manned it would show us the handbook with all the silhouettes of the planes he was trained to look out for, but I couldn't help thinking that I had seen more of them in my time than he had. Blackout was a much bigger undertaking at Malsis, of course, mostly performed by the prefects who would stride importantly into evening classes and pull enormous Victorian shutters up over the windows and drag black curtains across. News would come of Old Boys who had lost their lives and a few of the boys' fathers were killed in action which brought the war sadly close, but somehow in Yorkshire it all seemed very far away and I was too busy and too young to comprehend much of the history that was in the making.

One day we were all rushed out of lessons and bundled into a charabanc as it had been discovered that Mr Churchill was on his way to Leeds by train. We fell out of the bus at Kildwick and lined the fence by the track, and suddenly there he was, rushing by in a carriage doorway with his cigar and black hat and making the 'V' sign as we frenziedly waved and cheered. At least I think it was the 'V' sign though some wags afterwards swore he had got it the wrong way round.

I suppose I should enter the fashionable lists of those who write of the miseries and subdued inhibitions and dark complexes of boarding school education, but I must confess that, after the initial trauma, I thoroughly and healthily enjoyed my schooldays.

CHAPTER NINE

Parting Glories

Var. helice *and where caught*

L AUNCHING into a final chapter is like saying goodbye at a railway station. Either you have said everything you have to say already, in which case you have to spin it out agonizingly, shifting from one leg to the other, or you have to cram in all the things you've forgotten to say before the train pulls out. That is why I have left the rare butterflies to the end. They are all well separated, both in time and in space, and each has its story attached, for great events fix their circumstances in the memory. Everyone of my age can remember what they were doing and where they were when they heard, say, that President Kennedy had been assassinated, even if they forget the date or even the year. Rare butterflies come in two broad categories. There are the migrants, which you might find anywhere, more or less, and the residents which are restricted to definite, sometimes amazingly small, localities. The first are a matter of luck, the second a question of knowing the right place. I had quite a lot of luck and knew a few right places, though I shan't give any away in case the tribes are still managing to survive.

The Clouded Yellow is normally quite a scarce migrant, but in some years it can be found in huge numbers. It is a rich chrome yellow with broad black margins to the wings, and spans over two inches. The females are the larger with a few decorative yellow spots to relieve the black, as a lady might soften her formal attire with a little discreet jewellery here and there. They are related to the Brimstone, the Yellows being a cadet branch of the Whites, as you will recall. Not only have the Clouded Yellows a love of the sweets of the clover field, but they lay their eggs on clover or lucerne and so combine business with pleasure, unlike the majority who are only there for the nectar. They migrate to Britain from warmer climes in the south and though spring visitors may raise a brood for the late summer, our winter temperatures are such that they rarely manage to hibernate successfully, and we rely on climatic factors which cause them to move here when their numbers become overcrowded on the Continent.

Our first butterfly year, the second summer of the war, was a great one for the Clouded Yellows and we were surprised and disappointed when we hardly saw the butterfly again (it was not until 1947 that they returned in anything like the same numbers). The males arrive first by a good fortnight and fly strongly and at speed over the heads of the clover searching frantically for their ladies. Chasing a male Clouded Yellow as fast as you can run, hampered by the knee-deep clover, is a violent form of exercise on a hot day and, unless you were lucky enough to intercept one, a capture saw you breathless and triumphant like a wing three-quarter who had chased his opponent to tackle him just short of the try line. The females, in contrast, were relatively easy to catch, having no need to chase after anybody, and when they eventually arrived (we had despaired of ever seeing one) we found the pace less hectic, for the males tended to quieten down as well. There is a rare form of the female which is white instead of yellow, called the var. *helice*. I spotted my only catch of this in the grasses beside the kingfisher pool by the church one Sunday as I left after morning service. Of course I had my spring net folded and stuffed in my pocket, even under my cassock, and caught the lovely creature without difficulty. In fact I had taken it for a Large White and was idly practising, but once close up, I saw it was something unusual. We searched the clover fields for the var. *helice* after that, but only came up with Large Whites.

In 1947 we caught a male and two females of the much scarcer Pale Clouded Yellow. This is even more warmth loving than its stronger cousin and migrates from even further south which is why few ever reach us. That year was so hot and dry that in July the farmers were taking hay out to the cows in the fields. Our first I took for another white *helice* variety, but it is a pale lemon yellow and the black borders don't extend to the hindwing as in the Clouded Yellow. It is nothing like as strong in flight and it was something of an anticlimax to capture these very rare butterflies so easily. That was the year we went to join Dad in Hamburg and I was reluctant to leave such a marvellous butterfly season. In Germany we found the countryside full of Pale Clouded Yellows, though I was careful to keep the caught specimens separate from those we netted in Hertfordshire. I suspect they are not normally as common in Germany as they appeared to be that August.

The English Swallowtail is really the largest of our butterflies, with the exception of the Milkweed or Monarch which is such a rare visitor that it scarcely counts. Found in great migratory swarms in America, the Monarch has to cross the Atlantic to get to us and it is little wonder that few have been recorded. The Swallowtail is a resident, and our first capture was the culmination of a remarkable holiday in 1945. From the beginning of May we knew that the news of Germany's surrender must come at any moment, and excitement was mounting at school every day. Came the news that Hitler was dead and we thought, surely now, but still nothing was said. We were all making flags of the Allied Nations and hiding them, pending the great announcement. One of us hit on the idea of mass-producing little Union Jacks from blocks cut out of our india rubbers. Red and blue ink were plentiful, for ballpoint pens hadn't been invented, and we spent our lessons surreptitiously printing little flags on pages of our exercise books. These were folded double over lengths of cotton and stuck down, and a few miles of flags must have been ready. The news came just around lights-out on the evening of May 7th. Memories are confused but I can remember Bernard on the landing with a pillow in each hand and the whole pyjama-clad school joining in the most monumental romp while feathers floated about like a veritable snowstorm. Before breakfast our flags were up and the place was festooned with them, members of the teaching staff feigning amazement as to where they had all come from. More surprises were in store for us. We could all go home for the rest of the week, and Dad and Mum were actually on their way to pick us up.

We drove down the old Great North Road on VE-Day, past everybody's parties and celebrations, through mile on mile of flags and cheering crowds as though we were the cause of all the fuss. In those days you took the towns and villages in your stride; there were no motorways for the convoys and massive pieces of aircraft on long trailers would wind from the factories through town centre and market place. Down we went, under the smoke pall of Doncaster, out through Bawtry where stood a little café advertising 'Susan's Bed and Breakfast', dodging the market stalls in Newark, through villages with names such as Long Bennington and Great Gonerby (who could have been Regency Bucks) and on to Ermine Sreet (along which they would have raced their 'four-in-hands'); Georgian Grantham with the George and the Angel Royal and quick through Rutland and past the Ram Jam at Stretton, once kept by Tom Cribb, champion of England, who fought the famous Blackamoor with his bare fists, all cheering, all awag with Union Jacks. Through flag-strewn Stamford and under an arch of flags and on to Wittering where we would always start talking about Matron. Here the road was punctuated with Men on Haycocks, each one slightly different from the other; here he had no hat and there he had a pitchfork. Through Norman Cross and the Stukeleys and on to Huntingdon and Godmanchester, separated by only a bridge. The streets of Huntingdon were wide but the streets of Godmanchester were narrow so they didn't need so many flags or was it the other way round? On through the cheers and the bands and the laughing faces, past a flag-clad gibbet at Caxton where my war had begun, past Royston and the Heath and the Chalkhill Blues, and on and eventually home. At night there was a bonfire on the green and fireworks and dancing in the High Street and the King's speech was relayed on a loudspeaker at the Nine O'clock News and all in front of the Cottage. I was very proud of my dancing and I've never improved since. Lots to drink and nobody minded and everyone kissing everyone else and, biggest thrill of all, we were off the next day to Wicken Fen to look for Swallowtails.

I suppose Dad had planned the day to be away from the celebrating crowds, for after leaving Newmarket in victory dress, we hardly saw a soul. The keeper, a burly giant with a soft, countryman's voice, told us the Swallowtails had been visiting the flowers in his garden all morning when the sun had been out. Left to myself, I'd have waited in his garden for the sun to come out again for it had grown dull and threatening, but I knew the suggestion would not be well received. We had the whole fen to ourselves on this first visit and we heard the bittern boom, strange cathedral sound, but never saw one. A pair of Montagu's harriers were nesting on the ground. The male brought his prey above the nest and dropped it with a scream; his mate rose from the ground and caught it in the air, returning with it to the nest and her chicks. The fens are marvellous for birds nesting. There are so few trees that every one has a nest in it. Yellow wagtails I remember, looking like canaries against the black soil of the drained bogs. The sun shone only fitfully but just as I was beginning to lose all hope, over the sedge and reed maces at the edge of a dyke sailed a beautiful Swallowtail. It was in the net before I knew I had reacted. A large, perfect female and I have it in my collection yet. Tim caught a male a little later, rather tattered but who cared – we had our Swallowtails and the war was over in Europe and the world was a wonderful place.

Why the Swallowtail in England is restricted to the fens is hard to understand. It has become rare because of drainage and reclamation of the marshland, but its food-plant is not dependent on the habitat. The caterpillars in the wild feed on the milk parsley, but in captivity they will live quite happily on wild carrot or even the garden variety, though you have to be sure they haven't been sprayed against insect pests. Maybe the butterfly doesn't realize there is an acceptable substitute to lay her eggs on.

The next time we went to Wicken we took the Rector with us who had never caught a Swallowtail. It was August. He was charmed with our friend the keeper who told us that we wouldn't find any butterflies because it was too late and they had all 'chrysalled up'. I think he'd got the life cycle rather backwards but what a lovely new word! 'Pupate' was pompous and 'change into a chrysalid' was a mouthful. 'Chrysal up' was just right, and we adopted it forthwith. The Rector enjoyed his lunchtime bottle of beer and found the first caterpillar that day and we all found one or two, including a young one which would have been ignored, but I had done my homework and knew there was a juvenile stage which looked quite unlike the full-grown larva but gave a creditable imitation of a bird dropping. Full grown, he is a handsome chap, hairless and a bright yellow-green with a band of black broken with orange patches on each segment. The caterpillar has a strange protective device: when alarmed it pushes out an orange, V-shaped structure from above the head which gives off an orange peel smell. It resembles the sort of signal given by alarmed taxi drivers. As the Swallowtail caterpillar is about as placid a fellow as you could meet, the device is not often in evidence, but sometimes when I took the lid off the breeding cage clumsily they would all give me their victory salutations.

The Rector, Dr Greenham (he was a Doctor of Divinity like in 'Pirates', not the brand we were more familiar with), came from the Isle of Wight, where he returned shortly after the war ended to be vicar of his old parish, and I sang in his choir whenever I went to stay. He and his brother were the self-appointed guardians of a colony of rare little butterflies which thrived on a sunny, grassy slope nearby, the Glanville Fritillaries. Typical of the small Fritillaries, the underside is more characteristic than the upper, though the dice-box spots merge to form more of a square lattice in this species. Under the hindwing is a bright marbled effect of cream and orange in loops etched with black, like the endpapers found in old books. Legend has it that the Isle of Wight Fritillary was named after a Lady Glanville who was very interested in butterflies. Because of this, when she died, her will was contested as she wasn't considered sane by disappointed members of the family. This was early in the eighteenth century so bughunting has been reckoned a sign of madness for quite some time.

Our specimens of the Glanville Fritillary were given to us, live, by the Rector as he had successfully bred many caterpillars. During the war the slopes in question and the southern cliffs of the island had been taken over by the Army and gun emplacements and pill boxes had appeared where the precious colonies were accustomed to breed. So, while on his annual holiday, he took a number of caterpillar webs (they protect themselves in communal tents when small) and brought them back to Hertfordshire. Here he reared successive generations, returning the adults to their native slopes but keeping a sufficiency of fertile eggs to conserve his captive colony. The caterpillars feed on plantain; though they prefer their native sea plantain, the more widespread narrow-leaved one will do. However, the feat was in no way as simple as it sounds. The larvae hibernate when very small in their webs. In the spring, assuming they survive, they leave the tents and live in the open. I remember the breeding cages were adapted to give more ventilation than usual, as the caterpillars like direct sunshine and plants sweat in enclosed, sunny conditions, due to transpiration, which can drown little caterpillars. I also remember a full-grown caterpillar, a little black fellow with spines like most of the Nymphs, which had elected to chrysal up on the glass of the breeding cage. As the glass lifted vertically in its slot, the chrysalis had to be removed from the inner surface, infinitely delicately with a palette knife, both to save it and to get access to the others for feeding and cleaning. Whether 'Operation Glanville' had been crucial to the survival of the Fritillaries, I cannot say, but they were thriving when I last saw them – some thirty-five years ago.

After VE-Day everybody was suddenly involved in Party Politics and I gathered rather than understood that Mr Churchill wasn't a permanent fixture any more. I painted an enormous poster of the Grand Old Man decorated with bulldogs and Union Jacks, saying 'Vote for the Man who Won the War!' and got interested in drawing caricatures. I sent some to Gramp who must have kept them over the years for they turned up a little while ago. They were surely copied from somewhere but they have a nostalgic interest. Tim, who later went in for political cartooning with a talented panache which I could never hope to emulate, was turning his skill to more practical use. His handwriting was always mature, even as a small boy, and his ability as a forger was unique. Aided by a friend who was the business brains, he would turn out sheets of 'genuine' autographs of the County XIs and later the Australian Touring Side and anyone who was in demand at the time and sell them for 'tuck'.

The war, of course, hadn't been won, and Winston was out in the cold and Roosevelt was dead and somehow things didn't seem the same. We all knew that the second atom bomb was going to be dropped, as the first had been given considerable publicity and the Japanese had been warned well in advance but still refused to surrender. Wild rumours were rife about the power of this new explosive and how a bit the size of a pea could blow up a house, but nobody knew what splitting the atom meant – it sounded like something you could do with a sharp penknife – and of course nobody knew the devastating effect it would have. The morality of the thing never came into it. This sounds callous in the extreme, but then it is hard to recall the prevailing temper of the time. Everyone was weary of war and the cruelty and the inhuman crimes which had come to light, and here was a race of suicidal fanatics who refused to stop though their battle was clearly lost. The terrible tortures that had emerged into the spotlight of the Burma Road and prison camps in Singapore and Malaya, and the toll taken of the Americans in the Pacific Islands left nobody inclined to stay the hand of retribution if it would put an end to the conflict. We actually listened for the bang – for it was rumoured that one might be able to hear it half way across the world. No cloud darkened the sun and no sound was heard and it was all a damp squib. In our innocence we had never heard the name Hiroshima.

VJ-Day came and went with more time to prepare and more sophisticated decorations in red, white and blue, and by then we were home for the holidays. 'Uncle' Raymond Ramsay returned from a Japanese POW camp – he had been a doctor in Singapore when it fell – and was staying with us with a nippy little Standard '8' with an open top. He was dark brown and deep scarred and as thin as a scarecrow. Guests were mostly fair game to invade in the early morning, especially popular ones like this, and we found him sleeping on the bare floor with a log under his head. He was unable to sleep in a bed. We made a bonfire in the garden on VJ-Night and burnt a 'guy' which we had got up as General Tojo and all the children in Britain got a letter from the King in beautiful calligraphy on yellowish paper with a seal and George R on the bottom, thanking us for being so patient for the past five years. That was the end of the War and the start of Austerity and sweet rationing went on for another eight years.

Germany, just after the war, was where we netted an extremely rare English visitor, the Queen of Spain Fritillary. She is, in shape, very like a dwarf Silver Washed Fritillary, slightly pointed forewings with a downward droop to the tips, but it is on the underside that she wears her royal adornments. The larger Fritillaries, as I have said, go in for silver decoration like Major Generals at a court reception. Many things, more or less white or grey, are described as 'silver' – the hair of Old Irish Mothers, the steeds of idolized cowboys and the sand of exotic sea shores – but the silver of the Fritillaries is the real, reflective, metallic sheen. I once reared some caterpillars of the Silver Washed Fritillary and even the chrysalids, spiked and pointed like heraldic dragons, were tipped all over with burnished gold. Their close cousins, the *Vanessa* tribe, Peacocks and Red Admirals and Tortoiseshells, also have these metallic embellishments on the chrysalid but they are not worn by the butterflies themselves. The Queen of Spain Fritillary has more silver spots than any of them, a rare and dazzling display. Rich, not gaudy nonetheless – dull old Polonius would have approved – and I must admit that however bright our butterflies, they always preserve excellent taste in their own colour schemes.

Hamburg itself, though the war had been over for more than two years when we stayed there, was a chastening sight, familiar though we were with bomb damage at home. The people seemed piteously drab (we were never unaccompanied or allowed to meet them) though the children, many in rags and adult cast-offs, were without exception scrubbed clean and their pinched faces shone. We were told they used potatoes as they couldn't get soap. We would have liked to talk to them but even Tim, the linguist, was not up to the task, though he could make plonking remarks to the gardeners like 'It's too dry for the flowers!' We had to be content with grinning at each other instead, though many were understandably sullen. The city was still a heap of rubble, with many black crosses painted on the debris which meant that the bodies had not yet been recovered. This after two years. My chief memory is the tall spire of the Church of Saint Pauli, knobbed like a blackthorn stick, with five buzzards solemnly circling round it, balancing on the thermals rising from below.

In 1950 we moved to Eastbourne, where we got to know the Downland butterflies and would often make excursions by bus back to the Ashdown Forest where we had roamed during the war. We had visited Great Aunt Ella in Eastbourne in wartime when it was full of barbed wire and soldiery and the beaches were hampered with concrete blocks and forests of pointed stakes driven at an angle into the shingle to hinder any attempts at enemy landings. We had been as recently as 1948 when most of the defensive debris had gone, though the Army still occupied the Wish Tower and half the promenade. At the civilian end a notice said 'Cars Not Allowed'. At the military end a similar board proclaimed 'No Vehicular Access'! Here in Sussex we found a colony which we took particular pride in, keeping the knowledge to ourselves, careful not to take more than three butterflies in a season and anxiously searching for them from year to year for their home was never in the same place twice. The rarity in this instance was the little Heath Fritillary. Kirby called it the 'Pearl Bordered Likeness' which was not very accurate as it was more like the latticed Glanville than either of the spotted Pearl Bordered Fritillaries. The underside was also latticed, with little windows of cream and orange, again like the Glanville Fritillary but more rectangular. Another puzzle was that these Heath Fritillaries never seemed to frequent heaths, but flew about busily in more or less open clearings in woodland. Each year they would choose a different clearing.

The reasons for the rarity of this species were factors we could do little about, though we were careful not to over-collect, hence the secrecy in case others less scrupulous should come and wipe them out. The caterpillars were considered a great delicacy by pheasants, we learned, though our site was not a game preserve and the pheasant population was probably as small as the Fritillaries'. More important, their food-plant was the cow wheat, a straggling little plant with a yellow flower and parasitic on dead wood. The experts will tell me I mean 'saprophytic', but let it pass. If the undergrowth grew too dense, or the dead wood was cleared away by over-tidy foresters, the cow wheat would disappear and so would the Fritillaries. They would fly at the beginning of August, so a check on the precious little Heath Fritillaries was one of the first tasks of the summer holidays. The grassy spaces in this Sussex wood were also a favourite habitat for glow-worms, and we would bring them back and put them on the lawn at home where they seemed quite happy and would ornament the grass with their tiny phosphorescent lanterns at night.

I found the enforced exile during the peak butterfly months of May and June highly frustrating, and I looked forward to the days when I would leave Sedbergh for Cambridge and be free to do my own thing in the dog days. Sedbergh was very good for moths, but the butterflies were of the commoner varieties, except for a race of Green Hairstreaks on one of the nearer fells, of a deep, dark green, far more intense than those we used to catch in the Little Woods.

Eastbourne, too, provided me with my only specimen of the Large Tortoiseshell Butterfly, a weighty member of the *Vanessa* tribe, outspanning the Peacock and Red Admiral and reaching about three inches between the wingtips. It is not as bright as its ubiquitous cousin, the Small Tortoiseshell, favouring a dull orange brown rather than the brighter red, and has not so much black on it. The scalloped edges of its wings are bordered by a band of blue and black like ruffled braid which is quite jagged on the dark, tortoise-shell grained underside. Our books were written about the turn of the century and described the Large Tortoiseshell as 'common' which was cruel as the big butterfly was all but extinct. I'm sure it is powerful in flight for its closest relation is the Peacock and that is a strong and skilful flier. The last time I stayed with the Rector on the Isle of Wight he had one of these rarities, the only one he had ever caught, on the setting board, furry and supreme, a prodigious sight. From a window he had spotted a huge, dark butterfly on his own buddleia bush, rushed out with the net and caught the Large Tortoiseshell and half the bush at the same time. The buddleia still showed the scars. I must have vainly examined every buddleia on the island during my stay.

In the summer of 1952, Great Aunt Ella died. As the eldest surviving man in the direct line (I was seventeen) I was summoned from school before the end of the term to attend the funeral, the last real gathering of the clan. It was a wrench, as I was due to sing in an important concert and was just relaxing after completing my 1st MB examinations, but it was felt it was my duty to be there. On arrival I went to Aunt Ella's house, due soon to be our own home for some years to come, and in the dark sitting room, dead, on the drawn curtains, was a Large Tortoiseshell. I could sense her wry smile as my disappointment vanished in disbelief at my good fortune. 'There now, boy, are you glad you came after all?' The sense of her presence was as uncannily real as the undeniable presence of the superb butterfly.

Of all the prizes for the British collector, the Camberwell Beauty is surely the plum. In *The Aurelian* of 1766, the first notable work on British butterflies, it is called the 'Grand Surprise', which it certainly is. The name stems from the village of Camberwell where it was caught more than once at the end of the eighteenth century. I don't think it has been seen in Camberwell much since, but then Camberwell has hardly been a village in the past two centuries. It is really a native of Scandinavia and has a habit of hibernating in numbers in piles of felled tree trunks. Many of these must have been destined for export to Britain and I suspect, though this is pure conjecture, that some would have been brought up the Thames to Vauxhall and carried to a timber yard in Camberwell. When the beauties woke up they would be far from home and would have stayed around the district to immortalize the name of the village. The next year the same would happen again. The Camberwell Beauty is another large *Vanessid*, over three inches in wingspan, a velvet purple-brown with a broad creamy-white border.

I first saw one in flight during August 1947 in Germany. The underside is broadly similar to the upper so the dark wings and white border are quite unmistakable. We were on a river bank and Dad was fly-fishing for trout slightly downstream of me. There was a bridge some fifty yards upstream to my left. The butterfly sailed into view over the bridge, well above reach of the net, and as luck would have it, crossed over to the far bank. The stream was shallow and I could have dashed across. I wavered distractedly but discipline won. Nothing could justify the crime of splashing across a river with a fisherman concentrating just below. Not even a Camberwell Beauty. I shouted and they all saw it and I raced for the bridge, crossed and came down the other bank. Alas, lose sight of a butterfly and you rarely glimpse it again, and in spite of helpful pointing of the 'It went that way!' calibre, my Camberwell Beauty was lost for ever. That one, anyway.

Many years later I was staying with a friend at his uncle's in Cambridgeshire. The uncle was a benign bachelor with a large house who farmed his own fruit orchards. I gained some popularity with him by claiming a few Eyed Hawk Moth caterpillars from his apple trees, though the moth only lays one egg per tree, or two at most, and I hardly think they could ever constitute a serious menace. Neil, his nephew, and I had come to his quiet establishment to do some much neglected reading for exams. We chose a spacious attic each and would lock ourselves in every morning, slipping the keys under our doors, when the housekeeper would let us out at lunchtime. There we were, unable to escape, alone with our books whether we studied them or not. We even forswore the local tavern as the Ely ales were too palatable to be consistent with serious study. This must have produced a noticeable strain for the housekeeper, out of the blue, solicitously provided two dusty old bottles of her rhubarb wine which had lain in the cellar since time immemorial. It tasted quite innocuous so we finished the pair at a sitting. Forty-eight hours later when we knew we were going to recover, we decided the pub was safer and we resumed our visits. It was over pints in the bar that someone described the butterfly seen in a nearby orchard, and I knew that unless it were a leg-pull it could only be one thing. Amazingly it was still there and arose from the windfalls when I arrived with my net. It is one of my most treasured possessions.

This, then, completes the tally of the butterflies which I have come across since I first lost my peace of mind to them at the age of seven or thereabouts when I was 'nobbut knee-high to a jampot'. There are still fifteen left unseen of the sixty-eight, though I suspect it is too late for some of them. I will mention them briefly for the benefit of those who have been more fortunate than I or for those to whom the names are mostly new and unfamiliar and who would like a complete inventory of butterflies to look out for. To the latter I apologize that my list includes some which are no longer with us (I haven't had the courage to find out which). I have only described in detail the butterflies in my collection, those which I can put in front of me while I write. For the remainder you must consult one of the excellent reference works now published, for they are at once more numerous and more beautifully illustrated than the few we relied on as children. Some of our very rare species have appeared on postage stamps in recent years.

Of the Blues, there were the Long Tailed Blue and the Short Tailed Blue, both extremely rare migrants, the Silver Studded Blue which is not uncommon on sandy heaths where I have never been, and the Large Blue. The latter, now a much endangered species if not extinct, was fairly well known on the Cotswolds when I was a boy and is of the group whose habitats I have never visited. One Hairstreak, the Black, eluded me and again it was very rare and very local, though not too far away, in Hunts and Northants. The same can be said of two Skippers, the Chequered Skipper, which must now be on the danger list and lived in particular woods in the Midlands, and the Lulworth Skipper which was found in Lulworth Cove in Dorset and, as far as I know, nowhere else. Both the Bath White and the Black Veined White were extinct, though I have a fine specimen of the latter, a gift from a friend. Unfortunately it bore no locality label. The Large Copper was said to maintain a precarious stronghold in Wicken Fen when we were children but we never saw one on our visits. I have mentioned the Purple Emperor and I cannot claim it although I have seen the butterfly high up on the oak trees and met a man in a wood in Surrey who had actually found a caterpillar feeding on the sallow. He was (the caterpillar) a green svelte chap with two horns on his head for all the world like a jade slug. I would have given a King's ransom for the larva, but I was fresh out of King's ransoms at the time and I knew it wouldn't even tempt the lucky man anyway. I hope it reached maturity and hatched out.

The final group consists of butterflies which live in parts of the British Isles, mainly northerly, mountainous regions, which I have never visited. These are the Wood White, the Mountain Ringlet, the Large Heath, the Scotch Argus and the little Duke of Burgundy Fritillary. As Mum used to say to me at Christmas, 'Leave a few surprises for later!' I think it's time that I sought them out now I have some time to spare. I don't intend to increase my collection, for the urge to possess becomes less acute with the years. 'Cousin' John, who is now himself a bughunting parson, does his hunting these days with a camera instead of a killing bottle. A lovely way of doing it and I shall hope to do the same, though my old Braun Paxette is not adapted to such specialized work.

One thing I must do before I go is to bury the hatchet with the late W. Egmont Kirby M.D., author of *Butterflies and Moths of the United Kingdom*. I have teased him without mercy but we really did value his comprehensive work, which included illustrations and descriptions, not only of every butterfly, but of 958 moths, down to the Least Pigmy Moth with a wingspan of less than three millimetres. How he found time for his practice, I don't know. However, having paid my tribute, it is time to depart. I must not emulate one of our childhood favourites, the pitiful Melpomenus Jones, Leacock's curate who could never leave the party and eventually died in his host's bed. Instead we will leave the clover field, where the perpetual sunshine of memory stirs the butterflies, pass again the Six Trees, downhill on the path to home, evoking, as it always would, Henry Wadsworth Longfellow when 'The Day is Done' and three boys, like . . .

> The cares that infest the day,
> Shall fold their tents, like the Arabs,
> And as silently steal away.

Camberwell Beauty